the SILVER PENTACLE

AIRSHIP 27 PRODUCTIONS

Published by Airship 27 Productions
www.airship27.com
www.airship27hangar.com

Interior and cover illustrations © 2021 Guy Davis

Editor: Ron Fortier
Associate Editor: Gordon Dymowski
Marketing and Promotions Manager: Michael Vance
Production designer: Rob Davis

ISBN: 978-1-953589-06-4

Printed in the United States of America

10 9 8 7 6 5 4 3 2 1

the SILVER PENTACLE

By Nancy Hansen

VOLUME ONE

Table of Contents

To Kindle a Fire

Jordyn Orion

The vastness of space and time is immeasurable. There are alternate dimensions and parallel places, overlaps and crossing spots, wormholes, and intense vacuums where things are so compressed, the sheer weight of a thought is impossible to bear. It is not a place for the timid or the fragile, as are most mortals when confronted with their own transient nature. Only energy beings, who were once the spark and soul of life, collect there; filling in the little chinks and cracks in the great void between temporal events and dimensions unknown. And they wait... These ascended ones hover patiently, or not so calmly, biding their time with restless vibrations and glowing color shifts. Life that has experienced such a protracted dormancy often longs to be summoned forth to corporeal existence again.

The highest orders of those ascended beings were the Deities, those who held the web of creation somewhat within their command, though they did not engender it as much manipulate it to some personal benefit. They are the most experienced of the ascended, and are supposed to be infallible, all knowing, omniscient and benevolent, and of course they were not any of those things. Ascendance, like any other ladder to success, has its shortcuts and glass ceilings. Most of the Divine were at one time decent sorts, but just as erratic as the scores of mortal followers who persuaded them to take their first faltering steps into sovereignty, and then fueled their rise to power and supremacy with fervent prayers and slavishly repeated rituals. No matter how loved and venerated though, as ages passed and religions changed, the Almighty Ones fell just as easily into the dust and detritus of the past tense as the most humble forgotten soul. Yet most of those once hallowed beings doggedly hung on to the possibility of being worshiped once again, and so they still hovered in space and time, waiting to be called upon.

To comprehend the dreariness of a never-ending existence without any purpose is to become mad. That was always the problem of the idle Divine Ones; fighting back the howling insanity that results from empty eons of nothing more to do but mull over knowing too much about everything that ever was, or ever will be. The sheer boredom of immortality spent as no more than a long forgotten glowing ball of thoughts and memories gets old after a while. And so The Divine played games with those select mortals who did still call upon them, or shuffled around the positions of those ever-persistent entities further down on the power grid. They made sport of playing with all life, unsettling entire worlds, alternately encouraging and then demolishing hopes and dreams; creating allegiances and forging alliances only to break them later just because it could be done.

That is the sad truth of ascension: it is exasperating to have nothing to do but bide your time; and that kind of indifferent detachment from corporeal life always leads to mischief making. Once crossed over to etheric existence, one learns quickly it is absolutely more fulfilling to be a simple mortal working your way toward something better, than to have attained the top of the heap and have nowhere else to go. Mortals at least have the spur of finite limitations in knowing that a life has a beginning and an end, and so you'd better hurry up and fill the middle of that all-too-short existence with plenty of interesting stuff. Mortals always had somewhere to go and too many things to do, but all the spirit beings had was time.

Endless, boundless time.

~

The universe that humanity residesin is incredibly old. The light we see from distant suns is showing us events that happened long ago. Yet even knowing this, the night sky has a fierce beauty that is beyond description, for it is a panorama bespangled with stars as innumerable as diamond chips dusted onto a shifting curtain of velveteen folds. The probability of habitable planets orbiting at least some of those stars is high, but our introversion has always kept our attention primarily in our own snug little world. Or at least it used to be a comfortable place to live...

Amongst the countless galaxies filled with solar systems there was a particular one popularly referred to by its most sentient denizens as 'The Milky Way', for they could not see through the bright and thickly starred central area. Various other cultures in their cosmos had different designations for that rod centered, pearlescent spiral of stars—some of which were most unflattering. Within the thickly stippled coiling galaxy was one particularly bright star orbited by a range of planets and their

satellites as well as an asteroid belt. Life lived there on one planet—
corporeal life—watched closely by the energy beings most interested in it.
They clustered around it, biding their time, hoping to be called upon once
more, waiting for the summons to come back home and take charge again.

~

It was the third planet from that star, simply named 'the sun' by its
benefactors, that Jordyn Orion was headed for. Actually, more accurately
at this point, he was going to make a reconnaissance stop on its only
satellite, which didn't have any more poetic designation but 'moon'. He
thought that moniker quite unimaginative, but the humanoid beings of
the planet called 'Earth' never were all that clever with naming things that
were so patently familiar to them. For ages of their time these mortals had
thought everything in the cosmos above revolved about their own world,
and that attitude had persisted even long after they had begun to explore
the neighboring parts of the space/time continuum that surrounded them.

Jordyn was ascended too, and so understood that this kind of self-
centered attitude was handed down by former deities and perpetuated and
exploited by their spiritual leaders of the time for reasons of control. No
one wanted Earth's most sentient beings to understand their insignificance
in the greater macrocosm; not when they were easier to manipulate in
ignorance. Eventually it became their downfall, as each different sect of
believers held a dim view of the others' place in the scheme of things, and
the associated god beings pitted them against one another for sport. Wars
broke out, genocide became the norm, and bigger and more powerful
weapons were leveled from continent to continent, eventually destroying
all that wasn't poisoned or starved out.

The planet fought back against its now parasitic master species, and
eventually, it won. What had once been a successful diversity of humanoid
beings had now been decimated to mere handfuls living in pockets here
and there, scarred and mutated by cataclysms and internecine warfare,
environmental failure and neglect. Earth's upright and bipedal humanoid's
sudden downfall radiated shock waves of incredible force as the near mass
extinction sent hordes of suddenly bodiless spiritual beings catapulting
into the cosmos. There were far more dying at any one time than could
be reborn steadily amongst the scattered and tormented ones left behind,
and so the continual pressure of wailing, tortured souls milling about
overloaded the web of life and unbalanced the equilibrium in their area,

rupturing the spatial-temporal zone. The fabric of the universe was rent and torn around them, and bits and pieces of other places and epochs protruded in. On Earth itself, previously unheard-of entities and long lost beasts of ancient tales slipped through the malfunctioning power matrix, turning the once thriving world into a madhouse of total chaos.

Earth needed a savior. What it got was a nonconformist mid-level celestial entity that was flying under the radar of the Divine Ones to help humankind find the will to live again. Mainly because there was nothing else more interesting to do.

Jordyn had been forced to travel as essential energy, for he didn't have an advanced discarnate form like the higher vibration ascended to protect his passage over space and time, nor were there any worshipers to chant for him. In fact he was virtually unknown. He came looping down into the moon's weak gravitational pull as a glowing bubble of pure dynamism shot through with crackles of lightning beams in various hues. The colors of his life force varied depending on his moods, which were as changeable as his appearance might be, once he could manifest on some plane of existence. He stopped above the moon's surface abruptly, slowing his vibrational pulsing down long enough to drop to the gray, dusty crust pitted with impact craters. He simply needed to rest a bit, for the trip had been arduous.

Forming a face, he peered from within the safety of the sphere, contemplating the big blue and white ball of the planet ahead. It was mostly covered with water or vapor in various stages of development. He could still see land masses peeking out here and there that weren't obscured by nuclear fallout dust or volcanic ash belched out into flattened clouds, and that alone was a promising sign that Earth could still regenerate. Some of the continental areas had the verdant tinge of plant life. In the darkened areas there was little in the way of man-made light and so they must have slipped back into a pre-industrialized existence.

"So it's not too late!" His voice rang dull and lifeless within the skin of the energy bubble, bouncing all around him in eerie echoes. It had been a long time since he had used a real voice, and as flat and monotone as it seemed, it made him smile to hear it.

He sensed Luna as she pulled herself free of the moon's surface, and her own energy field globule bobbed over to join him. Her very pale and oval face, with the thick black lashes and silvery hair standing on end, was a bright contrast to the jet black and silver of whatever part of her raiment showed. The inside of the ball that protected her was filled with the weak white lightning slashes of her essence, for she was a minor deity at best and one that had been often ignored.

"I have not seen you in ages and phases Jordyn," she said cheerlessly, her smile sad and tight-lipped. "It's a mess down there. Have you really come to save them?"

"Perhaps," was all the androgynous being that was Jordyn Orion said. He or she—it was hard to decide today, for after all he had been both at one time or another—had no wish to share any more insight or information with a former goddess of this world than was necessary. Jordyn decided to be male for a bit, which tended to work better with off-putting aggressive remarks. Luna was always rather submissive around the male gods.

"Do you know if any other of us are down there?" he asked in a slightly more commanding tone, his projected voice growing a tad huskier as his features took on a slightly more masculine cast. He caught her in a searching gaze; his rich and crystalline aquamarine eyes glittering below downward sweeping brows and holding her wide and uncomprehending gray ocular organs a long few moments. Luna looked deep into Jordyn's being and saw that his soul fire still burned as strong as ever, and decided she had to answer at least somewhat truthfully.

"A few have come back yes, but they're scattered all over the planet. No one has manifested yet, at least as far as I can tell." It was not all she knew for sure, but all she intended to say.

Good! But she hesitates, so there is no time to waste. "I'll be on my way then," he said, and pushed off, his energy sphere rolling and bounding across the uneven surface again as it powered up and prepared to depart. He withdrew his features and melded back into pure essence before leaving the moon.

"Take care of yourself! The mortals don't seem to be very happy to see us," she added in warning, and then sunk back deep into the bowels of her airless metallic rock realm to brood some more.

The entry into and through the gaseous gradation was less than pleasant. All the drag and friction that built up nearly wore away the protective bubble's skin several times. There was no time to marvel at each layering of atmospheric density or rejoice over the increasingly hospitable levels of carbon dioxide for a corporeal being, for the thinning sphere that housed the essence of all that was Jordyn Orion began to burn off and it was not going to be a soft landing at all. Gravity being what it is, the drag was ripping apart the protective outer membrane of the last scion of Orion, and Jordyn struggled to hold it all together as he rapidly transformed. A mortal body would be a bad idea that high above the ground, and so he did what always worked before.

Jordyn flew; or more properly glided down toward the ground, using the last of his energy to become not much more than a whispering wraith-like thing of pure spiritual force. Once safely down, his mortal body reformed again, and became decidedly male. He gathered to him essential materials of the planet and molded them into protective clothing. He chose to be dressed as a nondescript traveler; that seemed appropriate to the circumstances of the planet. The last vestiges of his former non-corporeal essence were compressed into the small crystalline orb he called the Eye of Providence, and that got tucked into his shirt.

Taking up a stick for walking, he began to traverse the land, looking for those specialized beings he was supposed to find. They would help him in his quest to locate the artifacts that his predecessors—who were also hunters of lost souls—had left behind. His ultimate goal was to bring the spirit of hope back to Humanity, and in the process, gain for himself a far better reason to go on living too.

"Oh, I do *so* love a good quest with adventures!" Jordyn said happily, making a little skipping dance as he crossed a trackless waste of burned out desert filled with the blown apart hulks of war mechs and gigantic transports, all laying haphazardly around, in mute testimony to the large scale combat that had once taken place there.

Aleta Kalama

"You know that I am so very proud of you Aleta," Oriana Kalama said quietly, her brown, broad face showing the fine lines around the eyes and mouth indicating middle age and far too many long hours of work and worry about her family. She smoothed the lustrous black hair over her daughter's precious head, and set the headpiece of colorful bridal flowers in place. "Not many your age would have the courage to wed such a one as Samanya. You will be a beautiful bride."

"I love our people Mother," was all the small, intense younger woman would say, her voice light and equally as soft, so as not to show how anxious she was at the thought. In spite of her mother's gentle tone and reassuring smile, Aleta could feel the older woman's deft fingers shaking as she helped her dress and do her hair, and if she looked closely enough, there was anguish and despair in the unshed tears that made Oriana's dark eyes glitter so brightly. Aleta was the frail middle daughter in a family too large to feed well, raised in a small tribal society that was an amalgam of what were once races and ethnicities, living in a harsh world far too short on resources. The young woman had volunteered to be the bride of the demigod who guarded their village, protecting it from the metallic giants who shot light beams at one another and stomped down on those foragers who could not run away fast enough. Unlike many other such villages, Aleta's had been spared from the war of Almighty Ones as well as the spotted sickness that came with the big spreading clouds in the distance, the ones that brought blinding fire and dust that rained from the sky.

Samanya the Fierce and Unknowable had protected them from those things which had killed off so many other humans, and all he asked in return was to have a clean, chaste, healthy bride once every generation. It was a small price to pay for the survival of an entire village.

It was the most frightening thing Aleta had ever contemplated in her short life, and she had seen horrors beyond belief. Yet she dared not show her mother her fear, and the more Oriana fussed over her, the harder it was becoming to leave her behind. It was time to get on with it.

"Enough Mother, I am ready to meet my husband," Aleta said quietly but firmly, pushing her beloved parent's gnarled hands away while fighting back her own rising panic and despair.

Oriana pulled her daughter close to her heart, kissed her brow, and then backed off. She looked at the young woman one last time, and nodded sadly. A mother could never be prepared for this, no matter how necessary it was. For all her illnesses, Aleta was a lovely girl; so delicate and fine boned, small busted and thin hipped with rich brown skin and full red bow lips, and deep-set eyes that were often pensive, as if she saw things no one else could. She had the sweetest and most timid disposition of all her children. Oriana had been shocked when the call had gone out for this generation's bride of the god and her middle child had quietly stepped forward.

Aleta stood fidgeting a bit as her mother appraised her bridal dress of whitened sackcloth accented with shell stitching. She had been given many gifts by the other women: wooden carved bracelets, glass bead necklace strands, a crown of veldt flowers, and turned wooden hair sticks. Her small, brown feet were bare, the soles rubbed with red stone dust to simulate the fire walk. Aleta was ready to give herself to Samanya. Oriana was not ready to give her up, but knew she must. What was offered could not be withdrawn, or so the shaman said. Not without insulting Samanya.

"I love you with all my heart and soul Aleta. Now, go meet your husband," the mother said with downcast eyes to hide the sorrowful tears that betrayed her at last, and she turned and walked away quickly before she lost her nerve and spirited her daughter away to the wastelands, to try their luck on their own. Guiltily, Oriana wished it could be another girl, and not her own flesh and blood, but it was too late for that now.

Every person in the village gathered to watch as the drums started their beat, and the shaman shook the rattles, calling forth whatever ghosts and ancestral spirits that might want to witness this wedding. The villagers watching were a motley group thrown together by circumstances, with no conformity or unity other than that of being survivors of a great human holocaust. From what was left of their collective humanity, they had formed a loose society, with a couple of generations of warfare and its genocide component having washed away any sense of racial, cultural, or ethnic diversity.

Women of all shapes, sizes and hues ululated together, and their equally diverse men stomped a rhythm around the sacred hearth fire, dancing first one way, then another, the sweat standing out in beads on their mostly naked bodies. Young children stood round-eyed and wondering next to elders with stark and hopeless eyes that had seen every type of hardship and atrocity. Many of those elders mumbled half-remembered prayers. But every heart lifted, as small and lovely Aleta Kalama came forward from the bridal shelter; her thin arms akimbo, her feet tapping and stepping the rhythm of the bridal dance, the movement jingling the bells on her ankles. She lifted her sharp little chin proudly, dark eyes fixed on the heavens above from whence came the gods of old and their salvation, as she pranced and swayed her lonely way down the trail to the place where the great cliff their village was built on was rent by forces of Nature far older than humankind. It was here that handsome Samanya would come forth to meet her, and they would be joined in wedded bliss.

The drums beat faster and louder. From that cleft, deep within the rocky bowels of the dying Earth Mother that still somehow gave them life, water, and food—a rumbling began. The bridegroom awakened, and the pounding of the hide drums bringing him forth grew louder and more fervent. As Aleta drew closer, she could hear the sound of scraping and dragging as he pulled himself upward from beneath, a single step at a time. From behind her came the sound of gasps which were quickly covered by even louder music as a haze of smoke and steam issued forth, announcing to all that mighty Samanya was coming to the surface to meet his bride.

Aleta was trembling fiercely now, her slight form wavering on the wooden bride's bridge which spanned the chasm, her small hands tightly gripping the vine decorated rails to keep from letting the dizziness of her spinning head and pounding heart cause her to fall to her death and cheat her husband-to-be. She could clearly hear dragging noises, and with that the distinct sound of climbing. Samanya was almost there…

Behind her, a huge head full of spikes crested the top of the chasm, rising up above her on a long neck. It swayed from side to side in time to the drums, the glowing amber eyes with their slitted pupils following her every movement. Aleta could feel his hot breath on her back. She didn't dare turn around; for she knew she would faint in fright and dishonor her people. Instead she spoke, her voice shaking at first but then growing steady with resolve.

"Hail Samanya, Lord of the Unknown Fires, come meet your bride," she said in a clear voice, keeping her eyes clamped shut as she heard him pull his great bulk from the chasm to stand straddling each side. "Now give me your warm embrace to seal the bond, and we shall be as one."

The beast stood many times taller than her. Samanya was long of body, heavily scaled, with a spine-ridged back, and a long, thick tail that lashed the ground, sending small rocks and rubble tumbling into the chasm. A pair of coppery wings sprouted from his shoulders, and thick legs like tree trunks were ribbed and corded with muscles. Each of his two fore limbs were tipped by talon-like claws that advanced and retracted in his excitement. He dipped his head down and snuffled at her, and then reared back up again.

"And so you wish to wed me?" he asked in a voice both deep and hollow, like the booming of thunder heard deep in a cave. "Aren't you afraid of what that means?"

"I am afraid, but I still do wish to wed you if it will help my people," Aleta said barely audibly, her head bowed and her eyes tightly shut. She trembled, but stood her ground.

"Oh, I like that, it is an honest answer. Then gaze on me, fair one," he said with a hearty laugh that blew hot gusts of breath over her. She turned slowly, but kept her eyes downcast and tightly shut until he dipped one claw down to lift her head.

Aleta opened her eyes and quailed with fear and revulsion, for this was a monster beyond her wildest fears. And yet the voice had the gentleness of a kindly grandfather, and she could see upon his chin some white wisps of hair.

"Well, now that you know your husband," Samanya said, his voice growing low and softer as he bent forward, and his huge muzzle came down to her level, "Have you changed your mind?" When she shook her head, too speechless to answer, he viewed her with first one golden eye, and then another, tilting his great head like a huge bird. "You are one of the most delicate brides I've ever taken, but there is something very durable within. So tell me, do you truly want only to be my bride, knowing that to do so you will simply perish? Or would you want to live on, and help more than just your own village?"

Samanya was known for his riddling speech. Aleta thought carefully for a moment, and looked back at her village. The drums had stopped; the people stood and just stared in awed terror. They were a motley group as were most humans these days: dark, light, and all shades in-between. Young and old, tall and short, thin and rounded, hairy and mostly bald, they had come together from all over what was left of the lands beyond to make a small community here, with Samanya the Fiery to protect them. They were the only people she had ever known, and she loved them fiercely.

"I want to help people everywhere who survive," Aleta said quietly to the giant creature towering over her. "I want to help all that I can. We... we are so few now."

Samanya nodded. "How noble this bride is. Do you understand what is entailed? You will die here today, little one; and be reborn far differently than what you are now. Think carefully, it is not a pleasant way, and it brings the pain of self-knowledge and bitter memory that does not end. You can never come back and be what you were. You can never be a simple girl again. Is that truly what you want?"

Aleta knew her duty, for to refuse might anger great Samanya, and who could tell what he would do to her people then? The thought of her mother, her brothers and sisters dying because she failed was more than she could bear.

"I want this, my husband, with all my heart and soul," she said bravely, frightened tears streaming down her face. They had no choice; the food was running out, the water was no longer clean, and regularly falling bombs were shaking the ground closer than ever before.

"So be it! Then here is your death, and it shall be your rebirth, as well as that of the land. Go with the flame, and burn off the pestilence, and forge for your kind a new world," Samanya said, before he reared back up to his full height. On all four feet, he had still towered over her, and she stood shivering, as his great head drew back on his neck, and his mouth opened.

Oriana fell down to the ground and cried out in anguish, for she knew what was coming next. She had to be restrained at the shaman's request. None could interfere with Samanya and his Chosen, once the pact was made.

There came forth an initial blast of fire as terrible and as dreadfully hot as the burning sun had been before it had been veiled by the muddy clouds in the often hazy skies. Flames as scorching as the fires that fell from the skies during the fiercest battles billowed forward from his great maw and enveloped Aleta's tender mortal body; charring it instantly. It hit her quickly and crisped her skin to flakes, burning away hair and the fleshy parts beneath, melting what little fat there was, cooking muscle and sinew and all the organs within. She was aware the entire time, twisting and screaming in agony, her body doing a frenetic dance of tormented death upon the flower entwined bridge. The wood of that bridge turned to ash and fell in cinders and embers into the chasm below while Aleta hung in the air, wailing and aflame. What was left of the girl was soon no more than charred ghostly outlines of skeletal bone which turned into whitened ash when it was caught in an updraft. That wind blew her ash and soul aloft, away into the murky sky; away from her people and all that she knew. Aleta's remorseful wails of fright and despair became the echoing screeches of a great fiery bird as the last vestiges of her earthly body were borne away.

"And so it is done at long last." Samanya was satisfied, and he looked down with kindness and pity on his frightened people prostrated before him. "Behold, a new day dawns, for I have given you humans back your fire, as did my predecessor Prometheus," he said to their weeping and lamentation. Then he slowly sank back into the chasm, back to the bondage of his long and tiresome life. The gods may come to punish him in time, but once again, humanity had one of the tools of fate in its hands, gripped by a small, dark-skinned woman who put aside her fears long enough to do what needed to be done for all.

The Wastelands

At the end of a long stretch of desolation, Jordyn Orion was almost wallowing in despair. He could sense the horrific waste of precious life that had passed from the area, and it was nearly overwhelming. So many dead, so much destruction, and sadly they seemed to have brought most of it upon themselves. He had been walking for days on end, and had yet to see so much as an insect. Not a living thing in sight, unless you counted those parts of the warrior mech units that still powered up. He had abruptly and almost brutally disconnected most of them on sight, ripping out circuitry panels, wires, and sensors. They were an abomination! The tools of dictators and fools, created to bring death and destruction by worship of a technology gone astray.

Why did the humans grow to detest each other so? Why couldn't they learn to cooperate and make Earth the paradise it could have been? Someone had seriously violated the secret Oath of Creation to teach them the skills to make that advanced a level of killing machines. It was likely some of the more easily bored Ascended who whispered ideas of how best to eliminate the worshipers of some other god-being into the humans' more innocent and trusting minds. It bothered Jordyn very much that the humans had started to build their most terrifying war mechanisms into some archetypal image of themselves; a monumental technological advance bastardized into something designed to continue eradicating impoverished stragglers from lands now bereft of all resources and so poisoned they could barely support life at all.

"And to what purpose did we engender all this?" he asked the empty sky, with tears of rage and remorse on his cheeks. "Why make it such a lovely place to be alive in, and then continue to encourage them to kill each other off? Was it some whim? Did you decide to make a sport out of manipulating a bunch of ignorant wretches you have never seen and barely acknowledge the existence of? Was it worth destroying their world and all the wonders of Creation that filled it? WAS IT WORTH IT?" He screamed to the ghosts and the skeletons and their now unresponsive gods, who were safely back out there in the emptiness of space. He screamed until he almost fainted from lack of breath. But no one answered, so he moved on.

As he trekked further, Jordyn Orion thought about how much he would have enjoyed being a human; to have a real body and a life with some purpose to it, of knowing his time was finite and soon would be over. He didn't understand why mortals still continued to do these things to each other in the name of some deity or another when they had such short life spans. You'd think they would have caught on by now that except for some notable exceptions, the Divine Ones were mostly callous and unfeeling, with the attention of a gnat and the morals of a greedy toddler.

"And you're really not all that different from each other now, are you?" he sobbed, looking at the blasted out human remains around him. None of the bodies were fresh kills, most long dead and mummified or disjointed skeletons. Other than being structurally male or female with a suggestion of age, and the damage showing hints about how they died, you could not tell anything about whoever they once were or where they came from. Entire histories had been erased in that cursed place. The spirits of these dead left lying there were long departed, and nothing remained but a bit of their organic composition. And so they all looked very much the same to him. "I wish I could have met you all," he said sadly. "I would love to have known you."

And then something got his attention, and he stopped to watch a drama unfolding.

Off to one side and probably only a mile away, an eight foot tall bipedal robotic desert patrol unit was clomping forward, seeking survivors to round up for slaves or culling. It swiveled its head turret unit 300° around, and scanned the horizon for several miles with optics that had thermal sensors. Jordyn was not the least bit concerned, for he still had the ability to mask his sentience and knew he would only register as a faded anomaly. In the dull afternoon light, it was a frightful sight to behold, a cold and calculating killing machine that was designed to somewhat resemble those beings who had built it and then died for their breach of Universal Law.

There had never been a true deus ex machina in the world of the living, but mankind wanted to believe in something, so in the absence of their gods, in the midst of strife, they seemed to have reinvented the once revered Golden Calf in those giant war mechs. And long after the last powerful gods had fled and most of Humanity had died out, those killing machines that still functioned roamed the battlefields, capturing or annihilating their makers on sight, because that was what they had been programmed to do. No one who had deployed them ever expected it to be their own people who died, but the ragtag remnants of human refugees had become so genetically mixed that they were impossible to sort through. That was just the bloody irony of warfare that has no higher purpose than pitting 'us against them'. Any human can die, no matter her or his status, and only the victorious survivors got to report the historical accounting and repopulate the world. Yet this time the war raged on, generations after the reason it started had been long forgotten.

Something in the near distance caught the patrol mech's attention and it suddenly increased speed, creaking and clanking over the sand dunes, while hydraulics raised arms with rocket launchers already in locked and loaded position. Jordyn stopped his endless trekking and musing long enough to watch, wondering what had gotten the scout so stirred up. There was nothing alive for miles around them. And then he saw the other thing coming from an opposite direction.

A gentle clinking noise announced the arrival of a sprawling SCORP mine sweeper, an automaton of an opposing military group. It tiptoed over a dune on eight stalk-like segmented legs that shuffled back and forth, front limbs down and level with the surface, the coils extended and forward optics pointed ahead. Its dorsal optic system was nowhere near as good as that of the scout mech, but it had superior vibration sensors and some of the best armor plating known to mankind. It had felt the bipedal mech unit coming on fast and quickly refolded itself into a defensive position—body held low, small limbs braced, and sweeper coils retracted to expose serrated armor cutting, snapping claws. A tail section periscoped up to curve in over the body, the needle-like tip already primed with a neuro-toxin mix in case the mech was accompanied by ground troops.

"Oh do get this over with, you two big lugs, so I can move on," Jordyn complained in a low whine as they squared off to face each other. He did not want to be caught in the midst of a battlefield scene and be squashed flat.

As if it heard him, the bipedal mech fired two of its rockets down at the uppermost optics of the SCORP with the intention of knocking out the control center. The SCORP quickly raised each claw and delicately grabbed the rockets before they impacted, and flung them back at the source. The biped ducked and the rockets tumbled past it to explode harmlessly behind, blowing what was left of the hull of a personnel transport to chunks and flinders. The biped jumped up and rotated its arms, firing pulsar burst lasers in series at the SCORP. But its armor was too thick, and the scouts weren't armed with plasma cannons so it wasn't going to cut through.

The SCORP meanwhile rapidly moved forward and clamped its claws onto the biped's arms, starting to saw through the outer shroud and into its more sensitive hydraulics. It held the arms up and outward while cutting off the extension stabilizers. As it worried away at the arms, the biped raised a foot to kick it aside, and the first kick knocked it sideways, pulling off a few plates and disabling a thin bent leg section. But the SCORP was a well-designed unit, and it held on, the tail section lengthening as its tip rotated into a battering ram. That swept upward and took out the biped's optics, and then the ball rotated down and became a drill that went into

It felt the bipedal mech unit coming on...

the top plate and damaged the biped's control unit.

The biped immediately leaned forward and went as limp as a huge toy. The SCORP let go of the useless arms to scuttle off to one side and around the back, and then turned, and with a series of whirs and clicks, raised the claws once more. Small cannons with stacked discs appeared between the folded out claw sections and targeted the control plate on the back of the biped. Blue bursts crackled forward, and the biped jerked twice and then slowly toppled face down with a ground shaking metallic thud, permanently deactivated.

While the SCORP was getting in its coup de grâce, Jordyn Orion was moving gradually away from the two combatants, though he walked backwards the entire time, something he was actually quite good at. It was fascinating to see one intelligent machine take out another, but also a bit unnerving. It was so coldly clinical, the only noises the whirring click and shuffle of parts and the noisy explosions, crackles, and whines of their weapons.

"How very sterile and pointless this has all become," he said thoughtfully once he was out of the SCORP's sensor range. "Like some great virtual game. Those two looked to be brand new units, and I don't like that at all, for it means someone is still making them. That must be stopped. Perpetual warfare is just this side of insanity, yet I don't think there's anyone left to tell them it's time to stop fighting. They just keep going because that's how they were programmed. We don't want whatever is left of humanity to become used to *that* idea," he decided, "or we'll never get rid of this mess they've made for themselves!"

How many fascinating ways could they find to kill one another? If they put that kind of thought into making their lives better, there would be no need for wars. Other than some outward differences in structure and arrangement, as well as ethnic, linguistic and religious preferences, humans were all very genetically alike. They just could not seem to accept that the similarities between them far outweighed the differences, and their attendant deities had encouraged that divisiveness until it passed all reason.

Jordyn understood what was going on with Earth's loss of resources. Of course their crumbling environmental structure couldn't stand up to that sort of steady demand for more expensive and complex technology, and so there became such great disparities between those who held the power of life and hope and those less fortunate, who were being ignored as they slid to the bottom of the heap. Such disproportion of basic resources only fueled the hatred of those who went without. So the dispossessed struck back, trying to take away what they could not have. Ultimately that led to building even more elaborate war machines to put down the have-nots' terrorist insurrections at the source, and of course in response, even more of the first world aggressors were killed off. And the massacres went on and on, and on.

"Until this is all they have left," he said with disgust. "A barren landscape full of nightmare monsters of their own creation."

He had done his research ahead of time, and while things appeared to be grim, he was not entirely discouraged. Not yet anyway. Jordyn Orion had learned from some of the returning god beings and lost souls that there were so few humans left alive or healthy that race, religion, ethnicities, nationality—whatever they were fighting about before—made absolutely no difference in the end. All labored to survive, and in that struggle found their common humanity.

He found that most of the elemental basics of life were missing or in short supply, for the land, water, and air were often poisoned, and mass extinctions along with environmental disruption had made it hard to feed the people that still lived in the most devastated spots. Several generations ahead, the entire species might simply die out by having too few healthy breeders and little communication between them, if they weren't wiped off the face of the planet by mass starvation, plague, or simply annihilated by the invaders from other times and places who were dropping in regularly to see if Earth was worth colonizing.

Such a pity too; for humans were once such promising form of life, though now even most of the Divine Ones had fled and only a few minor deities were gathered around, reveling in the continuing death and destruction like drunken spectators at a gladiator tournament. Jordyn would have cried for all humanity if he had any tears left. He lifted his head to the sky and let the wind sting his eyes instead, their aquamarine shade dimming in the fading light under the perpetually murky daylight.

"This place is just… abhorrent," he said with a disgusted twist of lip. "I am a fool for coming here, looking for signs of life in a boneyard for the damned. What *is* the point already?"

Well, he had nothing better to do for the rest of forever. So he slogged on, head down and heartsick, almost out of hope.

～

Once again the foul evening tempest had started, blowing the sand and grit around. Jordyn staggered on for a while, and then raised his head and sniffed carefully. For a second, he could swear he caught a faint odor of smoke wafting in with the smell of old death and corruption that hung so heavily in the air.

"Oh, please, please let it be for real, and not my imagination!"

He stood trembling, waiting; but yes! There is was again! The brimstone and dead ash parted for another tantalizing moment to reveal the char scent of fresh roasted meat. It was gone too soon, and it became impossible to see very far ahead as lines of gyrating dust devils scudded by. Heedless of the danger to his mortal-designed eyes and lungs, Jordyn pulled from his shirt the Eye of Providence, held it in front of him, and glanced through it, scanning the horizon.

"Come now," he said aloud, just to hear the sound of his voice again. "Long dead bodies don't stink of burnt flesh like that, and I know I actually did smell it the second time... There!" he said in satisfaction, zeroing in on a faint heat signature that was biological in nature. "Something is dying out there, but if so, that means someone else might still be alive!"

He tucked the orb back into his shirt and started to run in the sand, skipping lightly through the dunes, dodging the whirling sand spouts, hoping not to step on an anti-personnel mine or have an old pit trap open up and swallow him. Ahead he could make out amongst the bleaching bones of a myriad of creatures and beings, a crumpled figure on a bit of scorched white cloth, laying facedown in the soil. As he drew closer he could see it was a small, naked female, badly burned, but gradually regenerating. Already her skeletal structure was intact, and most of her musculature had reappeared; in some places skin growth had begun. He imagined her internal organs were repairing themselves, for her ravaged body showed some rudimentary respiration and blood flow.

In the Eye of Providence, she had glowed the ruddy color of the fire element. Up close, he could see it clearly, a blazing aura around her, bathing her body in the Wyrding Light that marked an augmented being. He ran a hand over her, above the body, and could sense the latent powers. She was a marvel, a ripple in creation, not ascended but no longer mere mortal, though still rather... *toasted* at that point. The light of hope shone for Jordyn at last, for this was one of the four elemental champions that were prophesied to be the saviors of the human race. Hers was the power of fire, which was the first downward point of the pentacle, the star symbol that stood for the unity of all creation.

"And I located you so soon!" he said happily, his glum depression of earlier cast off as he settled down next to her. "Aren't you a lucky girl that I just happened to come walking along?" Of course that was no accident, for he had wanted to find someone, and so he did. Jordyn Orion knew too much about fate to believe in accidents anymore.

As the wan light of a hidden moon rose over the dunes and the dust storms settled down in the chilling air, he sat cross-legged in the sand next to a girl whose body heaved and twisted as if she was still afire, and he crooned to her a soothing song of the cold and sterile cosmos he had traveled through in order to find such a being as she was going to become. The lonely Hunter of Lost Souls was overjoyed, for he had found the first pure spirit he had encountered in eons.

"Oh and she's just so... so dainty and perfect!" he said in awe, as the final little details of what was once Aleta Kalama began to manifest, and she drew the first shuddering breaths of her brand new destiny.

The Fires Of Life

The small, dark woman groaned again, but this time her eyes fluttered open. "Is this... the way to ascend?" she asked in a worried tone to the ghostly face that hovered over her. Her eyes were still very blurry and she had trouble focusing; everything seemed to have a red flare to it. "You don't look like... one... of the... seraphim."

"Oh I'm not," Jordyn Orion said quickly, and he smiled, which caused his features to glow just a bit with that nimbus aura that all ascended beings have. "I could never manage to be quite *that* holy. The Latest Scion of the House of Orion at your service," he added with a flourish of his hat and then giggled. "Oh my, I've made a rhyme!"

"T-that's... an awful... lot t-to remember," she said in a dazed tone. "What d-do your p-people call you?"

"Oh! Yes, that. Jordyn. Call me Jordyn." It was his personal name in this present incarnation; he had chosen it for himself because there was no one else in this era of the Orion Dynasty to bestow a name on him, not that she'd understand that.

"All... right Jordyn," she said as she struggled to sit up, though her head swam and her muscles refused to respond. "Can you at least... t-tell me where I am?" she asked with effort, for her tongue seemed stuck to the roof of her mouth and she was having trouble swallowing; her throat was so raw and dried out. "I thought I died, but... I guess not. I need water," she added thickly, starting to choke on the smoke smell of her own skin and hair, and then noticed she was naked. "And some clothing," she added, covering herself modestly with hands and arms in strategic spots.

"All in good time, Dear, all in good time," he said, hopping to his feet and gently taking her hands in his to help her up. "But yes, you're still very much amongst the living, and as for where? Well, I'm not really sure! Some desert area in the midst of a war zone I suppose.

"But enough about all that," he added, seeing her worried look. "Let's see if we can find the water first, and then if we're lucky, we'll find you something to wear too, not that you don't look positively fetching as is." When she frowned, and made as if to walk away, staggered and almost fell, he added, "Yes, you are so right, we must be on our way, because this is a dangerous place. Night is the best time to travel anyway, and we've got a long way to go."

She looked very overwhelmed, and Jordyn felt perhaps he'd said too much.

"Do you also have a name that you can recall?" he asked kindly, handing her his cloak as the only cover-up he could provide.

"A-Aleta..." she said uncertainly, her eyes vague and unfocused, as if she had to dredge it up out of her subconscious mind. "Aleta... Kalama."

He put out his arm, and she reluctantly took it, and a partially-naked and wavering Aleta Kalama put one foot in front of the other in her first faltering steps of a brand new life.

"I hurt all over," she complained and he nodded.

"You should, I daresay you've had a rough couple of days." Jordyn looked at her sympathetically. She had just regenerated, and it was going to take a while before the new body broke in, but he was not looking forward to explaining that because they absolutely had to get moving. Her elemental glow had died down, and at that point she simply appeared to be a petite, brown skinned, fetching young virgin without a stitch of clothing on, besides his travel cloak. Her lithe and slender body glistened with sweat but she shivered with the night cold of the great desert and so he wrapped the cloak more securely around her.

Well at least she knew who she is—used to be, Jordyn corrected himself. *So some of her mind made it back from the spirit state intact. Not too bad for one who was formerly mortal!*

"I really need something to drink," she said from between cracked lips.

"Then off we go to find you that," he said lightly, supporting her with an arm across her back, trying very hard to resist patting her little round and firm backside.

They walked on for over an hour before he found a water condenser cooling unit in an old courier vehicle. While the distilled liquid in it was far from pure and rather flat after being heated and cooled so many times, it was potable and there was enough to slake her thirst. "You want some?" she asked politely, proffering the hose she had sipped from, but Jordyn refused.

"Drink as much as you can hold, because we can't take it with us. Don't worry, I can go a long time without food or water," he said proudly. She shrugged and then winced, as the motion pulled skin that was still much too taut and new, and then went back to try and slake her persistent thirst. He wasn't worried about any stray bacteria floating around in there. If she became ill, her vastly improved immune system would likely take care of it immediately.

Still far off but gradually drawing closer, there were some ominous sounds. Aleta might not hear them yet, but Jordyn could, and he frowned in their direction while she drank her fill.

"I believe the war is coming our way, so we need to go now," Jordyn said a few minutes later, for all along he had heard the sound of distant combatants and now it was gradually heading in their direction. The mech scouts might not be able to sense him, but she could be another matter.

"You know, you're being very nice and helpful, and I don't even know you," she said abruptly as she followed him back into the night.

"But I've already told you who I am," he said petulantly, bending over her hand and kissing the back of it. "I am Jordyn Orion of the infamous House of Orion. My people are the Doom Seekers—in troubled times we cast about for those special individuals who are destined to be reborn continually until they reach a more enlightened state, guiding them on their way. So I am a hunter of lost souls and various oddments, champion of saviors and sinners alike."

Jordyn thought that was a fairly simple explanation, but she made a face at him, as if what he said didn't make sense, but he continued anyway.

"So I'm doomed or something?" Aleta asked.

He waved away the suggestion. "No, but your world might be, unless I can find three others like you down here. See, it's not your doom I'm seeking, but to guide you to your destiny."

Aleta shook her head slowly. "You're speaking in riddles, and right now

I'm too tired to guess at their meaning."

"Certainly not!" Jordyn protested. "It's all quite simple, actually," he reassured her when she turned troubled dark eyes to his. "I suppose you could call me a redeemer or messiah, but that's been done before, and frankly I find it quite pretentious. I'm just curious by nature and I can't bear to think of this nice little world of yours meeting such an abrupt end. So I came down here to have a peek around, and lo and behold, I found you right in the midst of chaos! So I guarded you until you were... um... rested and restored enough to awaken. Now I hope you will trust me long enough to guide you out of here as well?" He gave her an ingratiating smile, and fluttered his long eyelashes.

Aleta sighed. "I don't see that I have a choice, since I have no idea where we are. So all right, Jordyn Orion, where are we going?" she asked him as he stood by her side.

"That way," he said and pointed unfailingly east, toward where the coast should be, because he could still sense the star alignments even if the night sky held the battle fog.

"And what's so special about whatever's out there?" she asked him curiously.

"It's somewhere else I've never seen," he answered vaguely, and taking her arm, steered her out into the night. There were laser blasts behind them that were lighting up the night sky, and aerial bombs were thudding counterpoint. "Somewhere they aren't trying to kill one another would be lovely."

"I can't argue with that logic," she answered dryly.

They traveled on together most of the night, trying to move away from the sounds of the battles and having to pick their way carefully. Aleta found a castoff bit of canvas to wind around her body and tucked it in as sort of a dress, but her feet were still bare and there were sharp ends of blown off metal and blasted bits of thick and clear plasteel glazing everywhere, making walking difficult. They started seeing people scurrying away in the night as they got closer to the edge of the blasted zone. A few scraggly plants grew here and there, either tough grass or succulent things with thick stems, fleshy leaves, and nasty little thorns, and there was less blown-apart junk and more intact and abandoned vehicles.

"I know this plant! You can eat this," she told him, pointing to one of the succulents that had huge paddle-like growth on top.

"How?" he asked curiously. The thorns were small but had a nasty claw-like curve to them.

"Like this." Aleta showed Jordyn how to carefully pick the thick leaves at the base where there were no thorns and shave off the prickles with a strip of metal so that you could eat the oozing interior. "It's bitter without cooking, but it will keep you going for a while," she told him.

"Ooh, that is *nasty*," he complained after chewing a mouthful, "But you are a resourceful girl. Where are you from, Aleta?"

She looked at him blankly. "Not from here, though some of it looks familiar. I know of no desert nearby our village and our nights are not this cold. I suppose that means I will never see my people again. My mother saw me die... that will haunt her forever," she added sadly.

Her spirit must have drifted for a long way then, for Jordyn had not seen nor sensed any settlements in the area he had trekked before finding her. "Well I'm so very sorry, but I don't think that can be helped. Do you recall how you... died?" he asked her carefully, since she seemed to already know that she had actually perished. That information might help him pinpoint where her people were, which was important.

She concentrated hard for a moment and then looked very ill. "I... I married a... g-god who protects our people. But I found out he was a demon, and he had... he had fire."

"You were sacrificed to some supreme being?" Jordyn said with incredulity. "That's simply barbaric!"

"We had no choice!" Aleta said in a strained voice that sounded on the verge of hysteria. Her dark eyes lit up and glowed yellow and orange for a moment before they rolled back into her head. Jordyn whipped his cloak off her as her body went rigid, as if having a seizure, and she began to tremble and twist while her skin lit up. The piece of canvas she had wrapped herself in charred a bit and then slipped to the ground.

Screaming in agonized terror, she ran off, trailing smoke and red vapors that burst into flame as they hit the air, so that her wake was like the tail of a burning comet. It was actually quite an amazing sight, but Jordyn knew if he didn't stop her madness, she'd burn herself up all over again, and they didn't have time for another regeneration that night. As it was she could be attracting a lot of the kind of attention they didn't need.

He grabbed for the orb in his shirt, taking it out and letting his body meld back into it. Seconds later, he stood in front of Aleta Kalama again, the orb at his feet in the sand, holding her at arm's length and making her look at him.

"Stop this!" he said in a commanding voice. "It's not happening to you now. You need to listen to me. You don't have to relive it again. Let it go

Aleta, you're not burning anymore. You are not on fire; you *make* the fire. You control it."

She snuffed out and fell at his feet, sobbing and shaking. "B-but I felt the flames take me again! I did!" she whined, suddenly more like a little girl than a woman reborn.

"That's because you let down your guard," he told her, bending over to offer her a hand up, and grabbing the Eye of Providence at the same time. That got a hasty brushing off, before it went back into his shirt. "When you died Aleta, you don't ascend, you were gradually reborn. Unfortunately the regenerated brain recalls bits of what that last body went through. Your passing was... especially traumatic. So your new mind remembers more of it than the average person would once they are reincarnated, and some of that—how shall I call it? Some of that *thought energy*, is bleeding through into this world. If you let the fear of it consume you, it will go out of control like that. So you must learn to master it. We'll work on that later. For now, forget about it altogether, and let's just be on our way."

"You h-have to help me, Jordyn" she said in a shaking voice. "I-I'm s-so afraid!"

"That's exactly why I'm here, Dear," he said patting her arm. He motioned her to stay still, and raced back and forth to fetch the bit of canvas she dropped, and watched discretely as she wound it around herself again with shaking hands. Jordyn gave her his cloak again. "Now let's keep going."

Actually, her elemental seizure had moved them quite a bit further ahead than they would have been if she was simply plodding along, and he was not displeased about that at all.

They walked the rest of the night, Aleta mostly silent and sullen as she numbly stumbled beside him. To keep her placated, Jordyn chanted low voiced songs of the cosmos that had no real words, just sounds. To her it was just some background noise he made, for her mind was troubled and her mood tense and depressed. But Jordyn chose carefully and it was all harmonic intonations that calm and soothe, stimulating the delta waves that leave a body relaxed and refreshed, making it grow stronger again. And as they walked, Aleta began to step in rhythm with his slow chant, and she did gradually unwind.

~

By morning they came across a small party of wary hulk pickers going over a section of demolished machines, and convinced a couple of them to part with a bit of half rotted clothing and an old pair of sandals they had found, in exchange for some coppery bits of tubing Jordyn had pilfered from a distant wreck. Metals were always easiest to trade with, Aleta had told him.

"The barter system is alive and well here," he told Aleta happily, handing her the clothing and sandals, and taking back his cloak. He turned his back while she changed in the lee of an overturned cargo container, trying not to think of how lovely and shapely she was. If those kinds of thoughts kept up, he'd have to transmute to a more sympathetic female gender to escape the urge to act on them.

"Well, that's much nicer, isn't it?" he wheedled as she folded up the canvas and tucked it under one arm. Living without much taught one not to discard something that might prove useful again.

"Yes, thank you," she said quietly and then walked past him back into the open wasteland.

"We'll have to find shelter soon," he told her as the colors of dawn streaked the murky sky.

"So let's find some," she retorted.

They had walked another mile or so, and had actually seen some small insects flitting through the lightening sky being chased by what looked like mice with leathery wings. Jordyn called them bats, but Aleta said she had never heard them called anything but 'dracule'.

"We avoid them. Some take blood, and they spread madness," she told him.

"We should talk sometime. You seem to know so much, it intrigues me," he said with a smile.

"I'm too tired right now," she said dully, for his perpetually cheerful nature was beginning to annoy her. "Let's stop somewhere soon and rest a while."

He found a long-wrecked aircraft somewhat dug into the sand. It had been some sort of flying wedge thing, and whatever hadn't been scavenged had mostly rotted away, so that mainly just the composite material of the outer skin was left. That formed a sort of pavilion-like enclosure. The shady area beneath was delightfully cool and that was important, for the sun coming up would begin to heat the thick air all too soon. Inside, it looked like a well-used shelter, judging by the packed sand beneath. All the anti-reflective material around them should keep them safe from heat-seeking optics, which was Jordyn's big concern.

"We can stay here awhile," he said, crawling under and pulling her along with him. Sunbeams colored with atmospheric dust began to stream across the horizon as the day began. He helped Aleta spread the canvas and watched as she lay down with her head on one arm. She quickly drifted off to sleep, twitching and moaning now and then.

When he was sure she was deeply asleep, Jordyn crawled out of cover and walked free of the shelter, where the orange globe of the sun that colored the clouds but could not quite burn through them was super-heating the air anyway. Now that he was clear of wreckage for a bit, he removed the orb from his shirt, turned his back to the east and held it out in front of him on one palm. Swinging that hand back and forth, he squinted at it.

There was the war front, the flashes of battle showing perfectly in miniature toward the south and west, the direction from where they came. Aleta's land and her people were likely well to the west of that field of dishonor, but the sea was to their east and much closer. That ocean is where he needed to go. Perhaps a couple of Earth days' worth of trip on foot; no more than three if they didn't get sidetracked or waylaid.

"I'm sorry Love," he said quietly to her sleeping form, after crawling back inside and finding a corner to curl up in for a while. "But you really can't go home again. Your maker is likely long gone now that you've been claimed, and your people could be dead or at least fleeing in the path of this latest skirmish. I can't afford to lose you too. Not when we have an entire world of innocent others to save."

It was a sad business, deciding who would be saved and who couldn't be, and he cried one tiny little tear for the lives that would be forfeited when he took Aleta Kalama away. He shed many more for this pointless, ongoing warfare that had cost so many lives already. How foolish too that it was something that had started over the dwindling amount of liquid hydrocarbons—which for all intents and purposes now no longer existed *because* of the war. Jordyn doubted Aleta's people ever had much to do with that dark chemical slurry of long dead things that had captivated the minds and hearts of humanity as well as fueled their industry; but now here they were, multiple generations removed, still suffering for lack of them.

Such was the price to pay when the gods tampered in mortal lives; offering the incentive to attack those they considered usurpers, using the same technology to kill one another that could have replaced the petroleum they so coveted. Now their war machines could no longer be managed and the survivors in the battlefield areas did not have the means or the knowledge to permanently deactivate them. This was what always happened when short-sighted mortals were allowed to play with the sparks of creation, and it was far from the only world that had been decimated so.

As he was thinking things over with his eyes closed, a small mech unit, one of the long-legged and fleet courier types, went stalking by, and paused a moment just past their shelter. Jordyn was instantly aware of it and he sidled over to the opening to watch it closely, for regardless of size or design, the mechs all likely had some form of electronic communication capability. But this unit was just lost, and the dispersal capability of the aircraft skin made signals bounce off it in a weird way, so it was trying to get its bearings before it moved on. He watched it trudge away until he could see it no more. Likely it had been wandering the area for years, trying to find a base unit that had long since been destroyed.

"See? That's exactly why I hate this!" he whispered to peacefully sleeping Aleta. "Your foolish people have burned up most of their resources fighting one another over the last finite bits of energy that their already overtaxed environment could produce, and wound up ruining their world instead, creating monsters of their own design in the process. The pitifully misguided idiots running this war have likely forgotten a couple generations back what they were fighting about in the first place. It's just an ingrained habit now.

"I hope we find the other three soon," he said around a huge yawn as he crawled back to his own corner to let his mortal body get some rest while his nimble mind raced on ahead. He wondered what lands they would need to travel to in order to find the next elemental being.

"I do so love a good quest with adventures though," he said happily as his eyes closed at last. "But it's far nicer to have some pleasant company along for the trip."

Stoking The Fires Within

They had walked for endless nights, or so it seemed. The days they spent in seclusion, now and then finding a small settlement to trade for food and supplies, or catch a bit of sleep in, but always they left at night, when it was safer to travel unseen. The active part of the war was finally left behind, and other than the occasional census droid, making notes of who lived where for whatever reason, you would not know of mechanized warfare at all. Except for the hollow, haunted, and hopeless eyes of the refugees around them, that is.

"Oh, how this place depresses me!" Jordyn said one night to a mostly silent and observant Aleta. "I have yet to see anyone with anything to smile about."

"Constant suffering and not knowing where your next meal will come from will do that to you," she answered flatly. She didn't understand completely yet where Jordyn was from, but wherever it was, he had lived a sheltered existence.

This was a more settled area than they had ever been in, though longstanding wartime bombing damage showed in the burnt out hulks of the old style high rise buildings in the backdrop. A decimated city of ghosts loomed outside the current cobbled-together community that huddled between the great metropolis that was no more, and the actual waterfront. The crumbling concrete and brick edifices that were still erect showed sections of ripped-apart, twisted iron girder skeletons, blackened and rotting. The now ruinous heart of the downtown of another age had long ago been abandoned and it was going back to the wild, though it still provided a stark and jagged skyline that stood in mute testimony that at one time, this had been a major center of commerce.

And so it was again, for what remained was still a port, even with all the original docks underwater. Throughout its history, mankind had always sought areas with access to water travel as the best places to occupy. The settlement had no name now, as most no longer did, for fear someone would repeat them into the wrong ears and the warmongers would look their way. But it was reasonably successful, and no one was outright starving, and a few live births of viable infants had actually increased the population that revolution. If not for whatever it was that lurked in the old city that all feared and none would speak of, the people might have even been mildly content with their lives.

Jordyn and Aleta had been able to trade for some of the scavenged items they'd brought in. Both of them now had a nicer and more suitable change of clothing for journeying. Since they traveled at night, Jordyn had taken to wearing all black except for a white, collared shirt with some rippling lace that though it was a bit raggedy, he favored the look of. Black boots, tight black leggings, a dark vest and a long threadbare black overcoat rounded out his outfit. He'd found a beat up old black slouch hat for shading his face, but seldom wore that anymore because his hair had grown out tall and spiky all around and long underneath. Instead he used a grease stick to encircle his very bright aquamarine eyes, saying it helped with the glare when they were near the waterfront or he had to be out during the day.

The residents of that place did use some sort of phosphorescent post lamps that ran on a strange power. The area immediately around the lamps was cordoned off and it glowed with a crackling energy that made all sorts of small bursts of purple lightning in the air, which was rather disconcerting, and there were a lot of them interspersed throughout the town, and they tended to come on at dusk. Jordyn tended to avoid them as much as possible, saying they were unhealthy. But while he might be right about the glow, Aleta figured Jordyn just preferred the clandestine feeling of skulking around in darkness more. Her erstwhile companion seemed to be a vain person, for he often checked his appearance in any reflective surface he could find.

What Aleta didn't understand was that whatever electrostatic charge they were using to run things in that place was not just keeping those plasma lamps lit but it also held whatever prowled the darkness at bay. That current was also interfering with Jordyn's sentience. He could feel himself fading at times, and while he loved what the built-up current did to fluff up his hair, making him seem taller, the constant needle-like tingling of the rest of his body was downright annoying. Oh, Jordyn understood well why the nighttime streets had to be lit up so thoroughly, but that didn't make it any easier to deal with. It would be so much nicer for the locals if they didn't have to be as paranoid that those ominous things that loved the darkness and saw well in it could creep up on them unawares.

He glanced over at his slender, short stature companion, pleased with her transformation at least. Aleta had experienced a few more fiery 'meltdowns' as he termed them, where she was startled by something or woke suddenly from a nightmare and had spontaneously burst into flames. But she was settling into her life traveling with him, and had stopped being so emotional that anything he said set her off. She had traded her ratty salvaged outfit for a billowy handmade cape of some kind of softly draping red weave over simple slacks and a loose blouse. The leather boots she wore were a bit roomy and clunky looking, but comfortable and sturdy enough for long walking on rough ground. Her dark eyes beneath the hood had a bit of a backlight to them, and she'd begun to add beads and feathers to her hair. She looked... impressive. Enough so to begin using her talents instead of avoiding them.

"We've got to find a way to book passage out of here," he commented

Both of them had...nicer...clothing...

as an opening to his idea, as they wandered the empty streets late at night. "There has to be a way to pay for traveling across the water." That was a subject he brought up often as they wandered the nighttime waterfront.

"It's too expensive," Aleta said quietly, and she peered around with some nervousness, for her senses were always pricked in places like this. It was too silent, and there was a never-ending pall of potential danger. "We can just walk up the shore to the next village; maybe it will cost less there."

Jordyn tipped his head to one side, like a bird, listening to the rustling and shuffling pace of something or some *things* from the shadows. Every night there were noises that followed them around.

"Well, that's true I suppose, but I like the looks of this port, and they have reasonably large vessels that seem as if they might be able to actually survive a crossing." He indicated the sailing ships that ringed the harbor. "With good winds, we could make it."

"We still need too many salvage credits for passage," she reminded him. "At least two hundred each. And I know because I asked." The ships could not anchor in close to the shore because of objects down in the water, so you had to pay first and get rowed out to them. That also worked well to keep unwanted beings off the ships, something that had been hinted at but not elaborated on.

"I'm sure we could earn the equivalent credits," he suggested lightly, hoping she would go along with the plan he'd been working on all day while she slept.

"How?" she asked suspiciously, for Jordyn's plans often meant she was going to handle most of the difficult work.

"By doing something that really needs to be done here, of course," he said, stopping to let the watchers catch up. He suspected what they were, but the townsmen would not talk about them. They just barred their homes at dusk, and hid inside with fires going all night, even in the summer. "We could be their heroes and then they'd let us sail on board for free."

"Heroes doing what specifically, Jordyn?" she asked him pointedly.

"Making this entire area safe to wander freely again," he said, swiveling around to indicate with an outthrust arm the blasted out part of the old city. "Getting rid of whatever it is over there that makes these good people fear to be out at night and nervous about scavenging too deeply inside those ruins during the day."

"That sounds very dangerous," she retorted skeptically. She was getting tired of his ideas of what they could do to save the world. Aleta didn't care much about saving anyone or anything, she just wanted her old life back;

to be able to sit with her mother's arms around her shoulders, and talk about boys and the harvest this year.

"You have something better to do with your time?" he asked her with an arch look, one eyebrow raised and his hands on his slim hips, coat tossed open to show off the ruffles he loved so much.

"Staying alive for one thing," she snapped, pushing past him and walking onward, her wooden heels clicking on the rough cobbles.

"Aleta, you have the power, why won't you use it?" he called to her.

"Because it scares the snot out of me," she yelled back angrily and then began to run away, because he was making her furious by bringing it up, and strong emotion like that always made her lose control and burst into flames. It still hurt to do so, but not as much now as it was intoxicating to feel the fire take over. She had gained enough control that it no longer burned off her clothing, though it still scorched everything outside her body that it touched. Sometimes when Jordyn was out, and she was awake and alone in the middle of the day, she would light a little bit of flame on the palm of her hand in whatever dark place they were staying, and watched it dance and crackle. She was getting better at controlling it in small amounts, but the all-over body burn still frightened her to the core, reminding her of how horrific that first experience had been. Even thinking about it now, her dark skin beneath the clothing took on a slight smoldering glow and her eyes shone blazing yellow. To burn something, something that needed burning, would be so... *very*... tempting...

Jordyn saw that glimmering, and her incandescent eyes, and that she wasn't all that panicked, and he knew what it meant. *She's ready! Oh my stars in the heavens, she is ready to burn. She wants the fire now. We're going to get out of this cursed place after all!*

And so he chased her and they ran, far into the night, looping around past the old city, where the shadow beings became something even more sinister.

City Of The Living Dead

When the radiological war had first broken out, thriving cities and important commerce centers, like the one where the waterfront settlement now stood, had been targeted. The idea was to ruin economies as well as break the spirit of the opposition. Most citizens of the area had perished in the initial attack, and many survivors sickened and died later. Those who lived on were often chronically ill for the rest of their lives. Some of them did breed though, for humans in stress turn to one another for comfort, and invariably their offspring were never quite human in appearance or ability. A majority of them died in infancy or early childhood.

Many second generation survivors were human in appearance, but a portion of them had permanently altered anatomy. Those who appeared to be congenitally abnormal were shunned and outcast by the more recognizable mortals who did remain, and relegated to a primal existence in the old city heart. The war went on, and the habit of taking shelter below ground to escape nuclear fallout, bombing raids, the effects of the icy nuclear winter, and incursions of ground troops and mech units became ingrained. Thus a new race of mutated humanoid beings that preferred darkness and a subterranean existence was engendered. There was relatively potable water there, but never enough food, and so out of necessity and desperation, they fought amongst themselves and with their more acceptable neighbors for dwindling resources and eventually turned to cannibalism as a means of coping with continual starvation.

When death comes suddenly to large numbers of people, not all souls manage to leave the mortal plane. Some lose their way, and out of habit wind up wandering bodiless over the paths they took in life. Others who die violently and unwillingly become attached to their past place in time, so that their spirit remains imprinted forever on the landscape they last roamed, replaying its life long after death. And some more hostile souls remain behind purposely for revenge upon the living, looking to pay back what was done, or just haunting an area out of jealousy that others did not die. If the living still occupy the same area, those acrimonious spirits will do what they must to make their presence known, including possessing the minds of those who are most vulnerable.

The old ruined city was full of such confused spirits and malevolent ghosts, the wandering shades of people who had died during the attacks, or in the aftermath. Everywhere, all around, half seen entities twined and wailed. Cold spots were the norm where horrific events had opened a rift between the world of the living and that of spirits.

Eking out an existence among the ghosts and wraiths a couple of generations later, there were still scattered corporeal survivors who were just as tormented and malicious as their spectral counterparts. These living dead had little reason to hope for anything better than a speedy demise as an end to their physical torment. They were the shunned and unwanted ones that the war with its radiation and chemicals had changed so drastically that they barely resembled the human beings they had once been. In order to gain an edge on those who had abandoned and forsaken them, they began to bond and meld with those demonic spirits who still desired life and so had assimilated an overpowering animosity toward others who were fully sentient.

That anger and lust to punish the more fortunate infiltrated the broken bodies of those who had all but given up. A new hybrid of an old scourge was born of such unholy unions, and the monsters of nightmares and the tales once told in whispers by ancestral humans who huddled around the fires that kept away the darkness stalked the night once more. Their numbers were initially small, but grew as fast as their more natural counterparts, for they were not as choosy about who or what was allowed to be part of their community.

When the war was several generations past and radiation had died down to a background level, human refugees fleeing conflicts to the south moved into the area to make the waterfront their own, knowing nothing about the living dead. The first generations suffered widespread sterility or birth defects and mutations caused by their poisoned environment, but they persisted, for humans are an adaptable species. Those individuals deemed too impacted by their infirmities were routinely culled, for a starving people have little resources to spare for being merciful. Most of those individuals were what the average person would consider monstrosities; freaks of radically altered genetics, and their bodies showed the defects rather plainly. Some died at birth, others not much later on. A few were very human-like in appearance and fully functional, and so they lived on, finding and fighting for a place amongst their more normal brethren until they were driven away. As birth levels were still low, many were accepted at first, but when the mutated forms started to win out over standard human DNA, a great purging began as humanity strove to keep its genetic blueprint intact.

Some of those culled beings were simply abandoned; others escaped when they realized that their days were numbered. They too went to the old city of ghosts to hide, and found more of their kind there. At first the established undead beings fought with the newcomers, and the sounds of savage bestial hunts and battles filled the night air, making the settlement people huddle before their fires in fright. Over time the humans adapted whatever rudimentary technology they could still manage into finding ways of keeping the darkness out, or just stayed away from the places where the monsters of the night lurked. Eventually though, as more secure housing was needed in the waterfront settlement, raiding parties went into the old city during the daylight to bring back materials, and well-armed warriors were amongst them to drive back or even kill the frightening beast people living there.

All the revenants were forced back underground, into tunnels that had always run beneath the old city bringing water, taking away sewage, housing utilities and in some cases providing transportation. Between the forced confinement and past chemical attacks along with residual radiation, they eventually changed, becoming less human and more... *something else.* Skin that had peeled and scarred over became pale and scaly. Hair no longer grew thick but hung in limp and listless strands from mostly bald scalps. Posture was hunched and four limbed walking and climbing was the norm again. Eyes became large and round, almost bulging, with all dark pupils at night, and pale olive with pinprick centers at the rare times they were above ground during the day.

There they had lived for a long time, eking out a rough subsistence, eating any creature they could capture, mostly rats and insects if not one another. Until Samael came, that was the best they could do. But now that the Father Redeemer of the deathless was amongst them, they roamed the night above ground, prowling for any unwary and foolish humans who were still out after darkness. Samael taught that more than just mere survival was important, and anything that was not part of their kind was both enemy and food, and so that was what their daylight dwelling neighbors became.

Samael had once been revered as a death angel, the one who came hooded in the times of warfare and famine to stand on the hills and towers over the corpses, his eyes filled with lust and desire as the spirits came to him for sorting and sending on to their respective afterlife adventures. Over time as religions changed and people worshiped science and technology rather than archetype beings, he like the other energy beings were recalled, as the Divine had felt their ability to manifest on Earth weakening. During the great wars he had come back to Earth and watched from the shadows as the carnage went on and the bodies fell. He was waiting for his legion of the damned to call upon him, standing skeletal and shaking, barely able to keep his essence together in one place. Eventually people under pressure did call out to the war gods again, and someone remembered the name Samael, and he answered eagerly. He made some converts, and found himself worshiped, which helped spread his name far and wide. He now was fully formed, and sat on his carved stone throne every night, waiting until one of the runners brought him a report on who had been seen where and doing what, what projects of his had been accomplished, and how the hunt went. For now he inhabited that burnt out city and quietly marshaled his growing forces, but lo, Samael had much greater plans...

~

"Do we have fresh meat tonight, Abbadon?" Samael asked, his long haired head low between his bowed shoulders and soulless eyes closed. The scythe tattooed between his thick brows resembled the very real and well-used one leaning against his cold stone seat. He was deep in thought, trying to read the aura of whatever new spiritual being had been wandering around the 'above' for several nights now, but it wasn't easy. Whoever it was had shielded well.

"We have fresh meat Master," the pale skinned skeletal figure that had slouched in on big bare feet replied to him. It hobbled closer on knobby legs and set down a hammered metal platter of raw chunks of flesh, still warm and dripping from the butchering, then grimaced with uneven teeth in mismatched lips. "Very good meat too, just sacrificed within the hour." The blood spattering the front of the demon's ghostly white bony frame testified to that. The still engorged appearance of his nether regions told his Master how arousing the event had been.

"Good," said Samael with a hint of a smile, and he took up a cube of it, examining the piece before biting into the sweet forbidden bit of bloody red tissue that had just moments before been the soft muscles of a nubile young girl he had grown tired of. He had been toying with her for some time, but she no longer screeched in terror every time he forced himself on her, but only whimpered and submitted. Samael preferred them horrified, puking, eyes rolling and begging for mercy, for it whetted his ardor, and so after that last time he had turned her over to Abbadon for his pleasure before he gave the order to make her the next sacrificial meal. She had been barren anyway, many of the human females still were. He chewed reflectively and chose a bit of raw liver daintily with long, gnarled fingers, savoring each of the rapidly cooling pieces before speaking.

"So, now I will need a new concubine. Find me a suitable one, comely and untried, and hopefully this one will be able to breed. And distribute the rest of the meat to our people, so that all may know the sweet taste of the enemy without. Save me a bit of the best for the leaders. I intend to sit in council tonight."

"It will be done Master," Abbadon said and backed out of the dimly lit room. Samael watched him go, his eyes open and shining a sickly chartreuse in the semi-darkness of his throne room, which was in the hollowed out basement and bedrock beneath one of the older buildings.

Abbadon was a good companion, a leader of one of the first groups of undead warriors to surrender to his command. He was a skilled hunter; brutal, ruthless and bloodthirsty, but also intelligent enough to know they couldn't just walk into the settlements every time they needed fresh meat or a breeder, and take whomever they desired. Oh, it was certainly possible to do that, but to show themselves too often would be to invite a monster-hunting reprisal. And if they had to kill too many, the food source that had sustained them, and the breeders that kept their kind alive, would be gone. No, humans must be managed, Samael taught, and Abbadon backed that up by killing anyone who questioned the Master's Commandments.

Since the humans understood that fire protected them from harm, the revenants had to find a way into their protected settlement that would surprise them. At Samael's request, tunnels were being dug to allow direct access to their residences without needing to wander so long above. Once the fires were snuffed and the cursed lights went out, there would be no resistance, and Samael would become the dark leader of the most powerful race of beings Earth had ever known. No one could fight off an attacker that couldn't be seen, and he had witnessed enough of humanity's style of fighting to understand that they depended far too much on technology and not enough on fear.

"Fear is the motivator," he told the leaders later when he assembled them for the feast. Two more deformed babies and a sickly human elder had been offered to them during the month, enough meat to call a council of the wise together. "Fear is the master and the slave. You see how they give us whatever they think they can do without?" he said, lifting up a tiny, tender leg dripping with gore. "In time it will be their best, and not their least desired. We will not have to conquer them; they'll offer themselves to us, because they will know they must. Fear will bring them to their knees. You can't fight an enemy you can't see. They have their days, but the nights belong to us! It is the darkness they fear, and we are one with it!"

The cheering was deafening, for the host was growing by the day. To celebrate they greedily dove into the slaughtered remains of what had been living human beings only mere hours ago, gnawing on the uncooked flesh, poring over the choicest of organs and entrails, cracking bones for the marrow and skulls for the brains. The corpses were not people anymore, just protein to be consumed with no remorse or concern for the lives young and old that had been taken. And the power of their as yet unrequited lust to seek out even more kills filled Samael, making him all the stronger yet. He sat back on his throne and sucked a rib bone held in slender, bony fingers tipped in blackened nails like animal claws. His long, matted hair fell half over his eyes and he threw back the hood of his ragged dark robe, basking in the adulation.

His army could be built and deployed, and after defeating their neighbors, any humans left alive could be farmed like sheep or cattle by those who stayed behind while the conquering forces moved onward. Life was good. Death was better.

Confidence Is Everything!

"Try it just one more time," Jordyn urged her, and Aleta groaned.

"I have been trying, and I just can't turn it on like that," she said irritably, her anger giving her more glow than all her concentrating on lighting the fire would have.

"It's because you don't believe in yourself enough Dearie," he told her peevishly as she stomped away.

They mostly worked together at night, away from the settlements where they would not be seen or overheard. What Aleta could do Jordyn did not want others to see, for fear they would either be forced to leave, or that some whisper of her talents would reach their enemies. So they had been out by the waterside all night, standing on one of the more fireproof seawalls that was made of a mostly scavenged metal framework and crude slabs of concrete. He had been trying to get Aleta to safely light herself afire. So far, all she managed to do was glow a bit and dance a few little flames in her hands, but as far as an allover burn or directing the flames outward—nothing. Her ability to flame seemed dependent on extreme emotions, and at those times, her mind overloaded and she had little control over what she was doing.

It had been like that night after night, and Jordyn was getting discouraged. Not only did he want very much to leave that cursed place and head out over the sea to find more of the elemental beings he knew had to be somewhere on earth, but he also wanted to leave what had been their home for weeks as safe and secure as they could make it. These humans, he had learned, truly feared whatever it was that lurked in the old city— so much that they were beginning to almost worship the unseen things as gods and idols, which was not a healthy situation at all. Those who could not travel outside the area had begun to adopt a more superstitious tribal cult behavior, and that included placating whatever forces they felt threatened by. He and Aleta had been with the settlement long enough to realize that they had been abandoning their dying or severely deformed children, and gravely ill or senile elders, to the 'Fathers of Darkness' as they called whatever it was that came forth at night and took them away.

It was a practice he could not support, for it was taking mankind backwards in time, but so far he had not interfered with it. Jordyn knew there was a hostile entity out there whose presence he could just barely read, buried as it was beneath the layers of metal, concrete, stone and soil, and he didn't want to alert it until he was sure what Aleta could do to support him. It felt faintly like an ascendant immortal, but there were far too many other beings around it, and those were mostly in that limbo area somewhere between eternal and corporeal. That was problematic on many levels, for as far as he could tell the revenants' numbers were steadily rising and as a race they were very much the aggressors. Once they outnumbered the humans, these placid mortals would never stand a chance of defeating them.

"Oh do come back here and try once more, we are running out of time," he pleaded with Aleta as she strode away in frustration, wandering down a dock to peer moodily at the nighttime sea. This was one of the small jetties used for the rowboats that serviced the ships, giving them something to load and unload onto, though only in the daytime. At nightfall, all rowboats had to be back to their respective vessel by order of the ragtag naval command, or they would face being sunk by cannon fire. No boats came to shore permanently, assuring that nothing from the shoreline could reach the ships unless it had paid passage or swam well, and that was the way the fleet commander wanted it. His responsibility was to take genetically clean humans abroad whenever they could afford it and to make sure that no ill-born defectives left the area. The mutated humanoids' spread out of the radiation areas was a great concern, and not only because of the altered genetics. The viable ones had consistently proved to be aggressive and antagonistic at best. It seemed that sort of thing was being prohibited in many places, and any boat that brought them in would at best lose docking rights and at worse, would be scuttled or burned at sea. They would have to be very careful when they did book passage not to arouse a lot of suspicion.

"We can take a short break if you like," Jordyn said in a cajoling voice as he walked up to her.

"I'm done with this for tonight," Aleta said abruptly, and she stomped back past him, with Jordyn mincing along a short ways behind her. He never left her totally alone after darkness fell, for she was often followed, though he did give her the time and space she needed to think things over. Unfortunately this night she didn't get much time to think at all, because her fate was determined for her.

Jordyn's sixth sense had been warning him lately that something was about to happen, and that night it did. As he lagged behind Aleta a bit, there was a rumbling noise and the ground shook. He had to jump back when one of the glowing post lanterns burst with a powerful implosion that initially sucked in material and then blew back outwards moments later. That area went dark. The same thing happened to the next one in line, because they were linked in an energy exchange. And then the support posts tumbled to the ground right after the globes shattered. The purple crackles that passed between them winked out.

Jordyn hid himself behind a dock piling, watching and waiting, for something or someone was coming, and he could feel it moving beneath the ground.

Aleta was walking just across from the first lamp when it blew up and she went to her knees to duck and cover from the flying shards. That was when she felt the street beneath her feet heaving. A sinkhole across the way opened, and pale shadowy figures spilled out of it, some upright and bipedal, others scrambling around on all fours or even six limbs bent in strange ways.

"Intruders!" she screamed and began to run away, some of them galloping after her. There was a slight glow to her skin, but not much more, and Jordyn was disappointed. It was enough however to keep the pursuers from touching her, as it bore the unmistakable heat of a fire.

Jordyn now knew what had been terrorizing the humans. They'd had many names over the eons: devil, imp, demon, ogre, dybbuk, ghoul, troll, fiend, or zombie.

He knew them as Children of Baal, the godling created slayers of the innocent and the scourge of all mortals. Those restless banes of mankind were engendered in times of great strife and upheaval, for they were the ultimate of all pestilence, beings that thrived in conditions that would kill most other living things. And they were quick to spread their infectious brand of malevolence and misery throughout the surviving humans, corrupting all they touched with madness and suspicion. Entire generations had been lost to their influence. The way they were working together here made the last scion of the House of Orion certain that they had a transcendental superior. Jordyn knew that one would have to be dealt with as well.

"And it would be so much easier if I had all my powers," he said with a sigh. He hadn't had time to look for any of his family's artifacts yet.

He stepped out to stop them anyway; a warding hand raised with the Eye of Providence shooting sparks in the other palm. "I command you as a Child of the Starry Heavens, go away. You are not allowed here amongst the sons and daughters of mankind." Jordyn put as much of his essence into the eye as he dared, and it glowed brightly, sending out blinding beams of light.

One fearsome looking thing with curled horns raised its head and sneered at him, only slightly shading its eyes. For a Child of Baal, it was rather large, and very human looking—a human/demonic hybrid maybe? The thought made Jordyn ill. That was an abomination that should never be.

It spoke, the words stilted human speech, but recognizable as such. "Go away Star Man, and take your pitiful trinket with you. This is not your concern." It made a move toward Jordyn with a huge and nasty looking war axe as several of the multi-limbed things scrambled at him.

His bluff was called, and he had to retreat. Without all his artifacts, Jordyn was all but powerless against them. Just as they reached him he retreated into the Eye, and as a globe of energy, moved up and out of reach. He noticed that the majority of the demon things had begun a raid of the nearest human homes, using dirt they had carried in with them to put out the fires. The screeching, terrified occupants were being dragged out into the night, to be hauled off toward the city. Not too many of them, maybe a mere half dozen of the nearly three hundred colonists, but it was still a great loss.

As a quite passionate and thoroughly furious observer, Jordyn was most disappointed that no one came forth from the other homes to investigate or try to defend their screaming and violated brethren, though

he understood that was a certain invitation to death anyway. He could see
that hearth fires were being built up higher all over the settlement, and
could imagine the frightened, trembling figures that milled around them
in prayer. Yet they would not band together and fight back, not even to
save their friends and neighbors.

"Well, this isn't going to go on too long if I can help it!" he declared, and
pulled himself via the orb to where his erstwhile companion had outrun
or discouraged her own pursuers, as he knew she would be able to. He
reappeared before a sobbing and gasping Aleta, who quaked with a terror
all her own.

"Well, I see you managed to escape again, my little coward," he said
mockingly.

"I… I h-had to run away," she told him breathlessly. "They… They're
monsters! They kill people, and actually *eat* them, and now they can come
out here to get us!"

"So I suppose we should just abandon these people to their fate and
move on?" Jordyn had his arms crossed on his chest and he glared at her.

She shook her head. "I don't want to, but we should go. I could understand
them Jordyn, and they said the vilest things!" She was shuddering. "I heard
them call me a 'breeder'. I didn't want them touching me so I burned a few
and then I ran, and they finally just let me alone. I was just so afraid! You
were right; we have to get out of here!" She was upset enough that her eyes
were rolling white without any spark of fire in them.

"So now you know the truth of why I was trying to get you to master
your ability, but you still won't make an effort to do something with it,"
he said harshly. "Well, I have news for you Aleta; nowhere in this world
is there room for your kind and them too, and they also know that. With
the demon population on the upswing, there will soon be no safe place to
run away to at all."

She gave him a sick look, shocked that there might be more of them
somewhere else. "I know they'll be back again, because they taunted me
with that, but I can't help it, there are too many for me to face. I'm only one
person—what can I accomplish by myself?"

"More than you think you can," he said in a firm and confident tone.
Jordyn knew that if the changed ones had only thought of Aleta as a
breeder, then in spite of her flaming ability, all they really sensed was her
human side. That oversight was going to become an advantage in their
favor. But first he had to get her to cooperate, and then lead her safely over
there to go down underground, amongst them. Whether the monsters'

patron deity could sense her supernatural side remained to be seen; but one problem at a time.

"Can we please go now?" she begged, as the noise of the capture and subsequent slaughter began to fade away.

"No Aleta, we cannot," Jordyn said with anger in his voice. He grabbed her by the arms and stared down at her, pulling her mind back to reason with his own, holding her tightly until she was forced to look up at him. "We are *not* leaving now. We have to stay and fight, because we're the only hope these people have left."

"I can't fight ghosts and demons," she cried out, her look shocked as she tried to pull away. She was surprised that he was actually so strong.

Jordyn glared at her, the intensity in his aquamarine eyes almost making her head pound. "They're only flesh and blood creatures Aleta—old flesh without much blood admittedly, but still alive to a point. Flesh burns, at least theirs will. But yours doesn't anymore. You can bring the fight to them, kill them off, and set these people free."

She pulled away at last. "Why should I? These idiots don't even want to live! The sacrifice their unwanted babies and sick elders to those—those things." She shuddered at the thought of them. "Let these people take fire and go burn them out, why is that my job?" she argued, but then a particularly agonized shriek from the darkness cut her thoughts off. Aleta clapped her hands over her ears and sat down heavily on the ground, sobbing.

"Aleta," Jordyn said quietly as he sat down beside her, and pulled her hands into his, "They've all forgotten how to fight. They're dispirited, and they need someone like you—like us," he added hurriedly, making sure she understood she would not be alone, "to show them that it can be done. Or else all humanity is doomed to thralldom or extinction."

Additional wails of agony and dread filled the night air while the last captives were being dragged off, essentially punctuating what Jordyn was telling her.

"Jordyn… I don't know if I can fight them," Aleta said uncertainly. "I'm just a woman, I don't know anything about warfare. We mostly avoided it back where I lived, and Samanya—he was our God—he kept the mechs and the clone troopers away. All we had to do was appease him once every generation, with a bride." She closed her eyes again and her muscles twitched, remembering the fire that had consumed her body.

"And did any of those brides survive their ordeal?" Jordyn asked her pointedly.

"Not that I ever heard," Aleta admitted.

She closed her eyes again...

"Yet you did!" he pointed out. "Doesn't that make you special Aleta? Don't you see that you are here for a reason?"

"To fight monsters?" she asked in incredulity, turning slighting glowing eyes on him.

"Perhaps at times," he admitted, encouraged that he could see some response to his prompting. "But more importantly, to give your people hope."

She sighed in exasperation and got to her feet again. "How am I supposed to do that if they all just huddle in their homes? Who is going to see me?"

Finally she was coming around! "If we go out there now, we might be able to save some of those people they captured. Aleta, these settlers have been good to us, but they don't stand a chance of surviving without your help," he insisted, more troubled by the noises than she was because he knew they could make a difference in ending this.

"I CAN'T!" she wailed along with the receding cries of anguish.

Jordyn wanted to shake her, he was so furious at her stubborn refusal to be involved. The critical time for these people was now, and at some point the girl with the power to generate and control fire had to face down her fears and start using it. The inhuman screeching laughter and derision of the captors and the pleading and screams of the tormented humans went on and on, disappearing into the darkness as they were dragged away.

"Oh I just wish it would stop," she moaned, but he noted that her skin glowing again. Somehow he had to reach Aleta and help her find her courage to fight back! What would it take the move her to action? Perhaps he'd been too easy going with her?

"Oh, but it *won't*," Jordyn said in a vicious tone. "Not for those poor unfortunates that just got dragged off, and not for the ones that will be taken next. Right now it doesn't sound like they're giving up their lives so very willingly to me. Aleta, you of all humans should understand what it is like to have no hope. Your people—including your own mother—they sacrificed you to a fiery death, simply to appease a demanding god. You went to him on their behalf, knowing you would likely perish, but you didn't stop loving them because they let you die in torment thinking they were doing what was best for all. These people are no different than your village was; they're frightened beyond all reason, creating deities out of monsters and thinking that is the best way to protect themselves. This could easily be your family, your village—and it will be someday, if these kind of savage abominations spread throughout earth."

"My mother... I know she thinks I'm dead," Aleta said in a shaking voice as she looked up at Jordyn. "I still don't understand why I *didn't* die!"

Jordyn saw her eyes beginning to backlight with the inner fire and he knew he had her then. He reached down and lifted her chin. "You didn't die because you're stronger than anyone could ever imagine. You're still here because this world needs heroines and hope so badly, and you're all of that. Save this one little settlement now and ultimately you may save some other mother of a brave and powerful son or daughter from crying herself blind for her dead child. End this madness here and these people will never stop telling the story of the woman who brought them the gift of fire that lights up their darkest hours. You've seen how they've used their hearth fires and their static lamps to keep the beasts away! No one can make flames the way you can, or take it to the enemy as a concealed weapon. These people don't understand what they can do to attack those monsters, but we *do*. Show them that the inhuman beasts *can* be defeated, and they will learn to get out there and hunt them down on their own."

That seemed to get through to her, for Aleta was thinking of those monsters carrying off her mother and siblings and her eyes had begun to dance with flame colors. "I still don't know if I can call up the fire when I want to," she said uncertainly. "Those freaky things scared me so much I almost snuffed out when I ran away. I... I might fail."

"Aleta," Jordyn said softly as he took her by the arm turned her around to head back toward the settlement, "you need only think of every woman in this place as being your mother, daughter, or sister... or every man as your father, brother or son; and you'll find the will to flame." He threw out an arm toward the entire town. "All humans are your family now, and humanity is under attack by an enemy that wants to completely annihilate it. A family protects its own. We need to teach them to face down these monstrosities before they spread further. Fight for the ones you love, so that they will have a better world someday."

She stopped short and looked at him a long moment, and then peered down the street where the attack had come from. Finally she turned her head toward where sounds of sobbing and remorse filtered out of the houses of those left behind as the frightened people prayed that their household wouldn't be next. "But I'm still really scared. You will come with me?" she asked in a quiet voice.

"All the way. I'll always be at your side," he promised, and patted her shoulder.

"I'm sure I'm going to regret this, but let's go see what I can do," she said resolutely. She had given her life once before for a small village of strangers that had become a family thrown together by fate. Aleta figured she could do it again.

"That's my brave girl!" Jordyn said, and he kissed her forehead before he let go of her. They ran off together into the night, side by side, ignoring the tunnel, which was likely guarded, and heading back in a roundabout way toward the old city while dawn in the east over the water was lighting the horizon.

What Lurks Below

Samael was well pleased. They had brought in two young breeders with the first raid, and several older males and females that could be used in arena practice for training warriors, and then be fed on after they had succumbed to their injuries. The youngest female and its heavily pregnant mother were not worth bothering with because it would be too long before the girl reached sexual maturity and the mother was middle aged, so he had already ordered them penned, to be slaughtered for the victory feast that next night.

Their first tunnel into the settlement, now blocked off below ground to keep any retaliatory forces out, had been a big success, though they had not known about how hard the cobbled pavement would be once they broke through to the surface. Some of the heavier chunks had fallen in, and several of his troops had been injured, and one killed when a large piece flattened her skull. Her body would not be wasted; she was going to be part of the feast as well. There was not much on her, and she would be stringy, but his people were always hungry, and meat was meat.

He had left his throne and climbed through the rubble partially blocking a tunnel that led to the surface in the middle of the old city. It came out in what had once been a large cathedral, most of the grand building broken and caved in, but enough of the original structure remained for him to see what kind of hallowed place it had once been. The gilt and grandeur of the crumbled walls were still there beneath all the char, watermarks, and dust. Having none of his more primitive minions' prohibition against daylight, nor any need for regular rest, he was awake most of the time, and often liked to be outdoors where he could watch as the gritty dark night skies began to brighten. He enjoyed greeting each new dawn while standing in what had once been a prayer house of an almost vanquished enemy.

Last night's raid reinforced for them all just how easily their empire would gradually expand around the globe, once his followers had interbred enough with humans to become daylight neutrals. Already some of the newest hybrids had regained their subspecies' original fertility from the crossbreeding, and a few were showing signs of sexual maturity and mutual interest. Once they had successfully birthed others of their own kind, the humans would simply become their cattle.

It was ironic that the center of his present world was in one of the very buildings where the faithful of humankind had gathered so often to pray against him and his ilk. They were atoning for that now, for where was their all-knowing, all powerful god of light and mercy? Off campaigning somewhere else most likely, now that he had so few followers left on Earth. And with the back door left open, the jester had slipped in to take his place as the one to be lauded, feared, and knelt down to.

"We shall build our first temple here, and we'll have a great sacrifice to sanctify it," he had told his commanders before he sent them on their way. "But soon all of Earth will be ours to roam." Now he stood in that spot, smiling and shaking his head. It had been so easy!

Samael the Grim Reaper of souls laughed so hard that black tears rolled down his cheeks. The irony of the situation was almost comical. Humanity had fought each other into near extinction, and now the very thing they feared from one another was overtaking them from within. When his brothers of the Apocalypse joined him, it truly would be the end of days for humanity and a new era for its long forsaken bastard brothers and sisters.

~

Streaks of ruddy dawn had lightened the sky, as the angel of death was picking his way back toward the tunnel mouth he had come out of, when he felt the first tingling sensation of another ascended presence approaching. It came from just on the outskirts of the city, and was moving in fast.

He paused and tried to read it, but it was something he had never dealt with, and well-shielded. He had expected some sort of reprisal, but not so soon. The nearby humans had no warriors or weapons, and little in the way of resources. Perhaps they had contacted one of the ships and gathered together whatever was left of the decrepit soldiers that were aboard. They obviously had a high priest or maybe even a saint amongst them. No bother, they would not stand against him and his merciless horde.

The death angel had given up his ability to teleport or fly when he decided to become fully corporeal again, but he was not without tricks. Since no alarm horns had sounded, the guards likely would not have picked up on this other presence, for they could not sense its higher energy vibrations the way he could. Fortunately whatever matter transfer Samael had sacrificed in mobility to manifest wholly on Earth, he had gained in strength.

"Let them bring the fight to us then, we know this rat's warren far better than they!"

He moved swiftly below and called to his commanders to be ready for attack, and gathered his personal guard to his side. The elite group would make their stand together against the oncoming holy one in the wide central hall cavern that they used as an arena, and the rest would box in whatever other beings came forth from all around, until there was no escape except a battle to a painful death. It would be very entertaining, and then they would have a much more bountiful feast afterward.

"Last night we taught the humans some valuable lessons, for those pitiful mortals now know they cannot keep us out of their lives. Once we defeat whatever pathetic forces they are throwing at us, they will bow to us from here on in. Today they conveniently bring the fight here. So let us show them how well we can defend ourselves," Samael said in a raw shout as he threw off his cloak and robes and stood in the dark armor of the death angel before them.

"Strike fiercely and often, for we now vie for our right to claim this wretched world they all but destroyed!" He raised his scythe on high to a chorus of fell shouts and curses, as all around him, handmade blades straight and sharp, swords with curves and saw teeth, and axes both single and double-bitted, were brandished overhead.

~

"Where do you think they all are?" Aleta said in a hoarse whisper to Jordyn as they wandered the cold and whistling streets of the bombed out city. She could feel the clammy presences of the dead; for restless spirits still ceaselessly wandered the place, sometimes passing right through them, and it was unnerving enough to make even she who was never cold anymore begin to shiver.

"I would guess because of the daylight, below ground," he answered quietly, his head cocked like a bird watching for worms. But he was not listening as much as feeling, sensing the presence of another mid-level celestial entity like himself. Not really *like* him though, for this one had an aura of malevolence beyond any he had ever met.

They stalked the streets together side by side, seemingly unarmed. But that was far from the truth, for Jordyn Orion had defenses about him that he could not explain but could access when needed. And Aleta Kalama had a special ability—the gift of fire calling. Whatever happened, she would likely survive it if she could learn to control those flames. Jordyn's only regret was that he had not had more time to work with her. But he also had not expected to encounter another of the more meddlesome and ambitious ascended so soon. Now he knew why Luna of the Moon had been so evasive about who was on Earth. She must have known there were others of their kind staking out territories already.

"Now, that looks like a way into their realm," he said, spying a well-used stairwell down to the basement level of a building which long ago had housed underground shops. He slowly began to descend the cracked and uneven steps, keeping his senses alert. Jordyn could see well enough in the dark, but even without vision he knew they were being watched, no doubt walking into a trap. He was not concerned for himself, for he could simply vanish at will and throw the watchers off if he was threatened; but his companion was rooted to Earth and so he stayed with her.

"It stinks in here," Aleta said with disgust, as she followed closely behind him.

"Yes, very much so," Jordyn said, wrinkling his nose in distaste, for it was an abattoir reek. Only he could see the cracked open, sightless skulls and gnawed on bits and pieces of what were once humans, or at least things that resembled humans. Those creatures he had seen last night swarming into the settlement were not human at all, not anymore; but an offshoot branch of the same line, highly specialized for hunting and killing other intelligent beings. They had begun as an altered being designed only to hunt down those humans whose minds and souls were so corrupted they had been marked for extermination. They were a different branch of the genetic line, night hunters that were essentially cannibals, for they ate the meat, blood, bone marrow and especially the brains of their prey, all high in fats and protein, and their hunger was ceaseless. For that reason, they had been been granted only limited intelligence and short life spans. These demons had been killed off before, and yet they kept being reborn in eras of great upheaval. And this time, it wasn't Baal who led them but someone more ruthless and less interested in regional conquest than complete enslavement and eventual annihilation of the entire human race.

"It's getting impossible to see in here," she complained in a whisper. Aleta's still human eyes were taking longer to adjust than Jordyn's and the farther they went along into the labyrinthine series of basements and connecting tunnels, the more the perpetual gloom rapidly turned into thick darkness. She did not recognize the piles of gnawed bones and old offal that littered the place in heaps for what they were. But she could smell the filth and rot of dead things, and in the stale air it was almost gagging.

He fingered the Eye of Providence, because it was a comforting thought. Soon perhaps, but not yet...

"I don't want to risk a light, no telling what it will draw to us," he whispered back.

Because of the darkness neither one of them could see those things that were scuttling along far above them on the rafters and carrier beams at the underside of the building. The crawlers were watching and waiting for the right moment to drop down. Like oversize, pale spiders they sidled rapidly on four or six limbs, as perfectly at home scurrying around in that dark, dank network of man-made rails and crosspieces as their ancestors might have been on tree limbs in some great jungle. Large, bulbous eyes that were almost as much pupil as iris watched the two invaders below carefully, ascertaining that they were the only ones coming forth. Their orders were to track and follow, but not engage until the entire attacking party was inside together.

~

Abbadon took a scout's whispered report directly to his master. "There are only two Master, a female breeder the raiding party could not catch yesterday, and something that looks human but is not. That one also has the off-world vibration."

"Does it now?" Samael said with a sneer. So one of his celestial competitors had come forth at last. But which one? "Let them get closer, and then take out the female, the out-worlder is mine," he told Abbadon.

"It shall be done," the skeletal undead being said, and bowed, strands of dust-stiffened blonde hair falling over a face with leathery skin stretched tight over a misshapen skull. Abbadon had the deep-set feral eyes and the slinking grace of a natural born killer. He moved off silently, and Samael watched him go with great gratitude.

Abbadon was of the highest rank of undead that had been born there in the city. He could at times go out into the open during broad daylight and still see without being completely blinded. Even at his advanced age, his long, knobby legs were tireless, and his thin arms were surprisingly strong enough to wield weapons that would crush ribs and bash in skulls. He was a fighter from birth and had risen to the top of his tribe by killing off all the other competitors. The sons and daughters of the dark underworld that he had bred from the human females he brutally ravaged were uniformly fierce and warlike as well as capable, and most of them were much bigger than their sire. The death lord was glad to have Abbadon on his side. The demon would protect his master with his very life if necessary, for it had always been his wish to unite the deathless killers and take humanity out for good, though he could not quite understand that would be the death of his own kind as well.

"Go," Samael said to the few that had gathered to stand with him. "Detain the female and separate the out-worlder. Bring that one to me."

～

Aleta was having trouble seeing even a few feet ahead. She had stopped to get her bearings, and she was now several paces behind Jordyn when the first of the crawlers dropped down on her. It knocked her slight figure to the ground and snapped in her face, yellow pointed teeth gnashing repeatedly as it went for her throat.

"Go to Hades!" she screamed out a curse as she went blazing alight, her body's self-defenses automatically responding before her mind could even form the thought. She screeched in terror along with the inhuman creature as it immediately began to writhe and twist in flames that burned so hot they turned it to skeletal coals within seconds. There was a chorus of surprised and dismayed hisses, and the loud, echoing sound of several large sheets of heavy metal slamming down, and then… *silence.*

Tossing the charred corpse off her in disgust, she stood up still somewhat afire and alone in the center of an open space, now lighted enough to see that there were other crawlers all around her. Quite a few had dropped to the floor; some clung to structures overhead or against the walls. The nightmare things had eyes that were large and bulging, the pupils shrunk to almost pinpricks in the sudden bright light as they watched her with bestial ferocity. They seemed only rudimentarily intelligent, though their faces were vaguely humanoid.

Aleta spun around, for she now had no idea where Jordyn was. Maybe he was already overwhelmed and dead? There was no discernible passage from the room, so it was fight or die—likely both—for she was outnumbered by at least a couple dozen of the crawling things.

"Oh, you're not taking me that easily," she said shaking a fist at the nearest one slinking up. Licks of orange and yellow flame lashed out from her hand. She could feel the fire building now, her anger and revulsion feeding it, her mind rejoicing in that feeling of conflagrant power and self-confidence that surged through her at last.

Eyes glowing bright vermilion, she began to advance on the nearest ones, arms outstretched and crackling flames spouting from all sides. She thought of her mother, and her sisters and brothers, and all the people left behind in her village when Samanya took her with his flames. "We'll die together, you filthy, vile things! This is a message from my people, the human race, and we say go back to the pits of hell that spawned you!"

A great gout of flames flared from her mouth as she spoke and out of instinct Aleta blew them outward. The flames roared forth, shooting across the small room as the fire consumed her, and she burned to a furious roaring blaze, with hatred and anger long suppressed. Anger that humanity was making its last stand in a world they had ruined for themselves, hatred of the things it had allowed itself to become while those wars went on. Aleta knew now the secret that Jordyn Orion had tried to keep from her for so long. These things he wanted her to fight were also human, or at least at one time they had been. They were the living embodiment of the very worst of humanity, what happens when a people were corrupted beyond hope. If what was good and worthy about humanity was going to survive in that world, these demonic beings had to die. Wherever they were, the aberrant evil killing machines of creation had to be eliminated.

"And I'm the fiery death that will take you out of our world!" she said with glee and then started to whirl around like a dervish, dancing wildly as she had at her wedding with Samanya. Thinking of that time, she felt the flames crackling off her body, and realized they were now filling the room. The crawling creatures screeched and scrambled in a vain attempt to get away before the burning witch cooked the flesh off their still far too mortal remains.

"DIE!" she bellowed in fury as she felt the blast of the inferno reach an apex. It left her body and hit every wall, each nook and cranny, and the base of the floor above, setting the entire room completely ablaze. "Die in the flames the way I had to die in order to be reborn to kill you all in the defense of my people!"

~

Jordyn Orion had been allowed to become separated from Aleta Kalama before the rest of the undead horde bore down on him. He had just passed through a tunnel opening into another building basement when he realized she was no longer with him. He turned to call out to her when a panel of metal slammed down between them. The way ahead was blocked also, as dozens of bodies filled that opening, while more of them sifted in around him. He was soon surrounded. The entire underground part of the building he was in had become an arena-like battlefield.

He knew then Aleta was going to face the first test of her powers alone, as he could not easily teleport back to her. To do so he would have to pass through solid matter, something he could not manage without sustaining damage. It would be better to stand his ground anyway, in case Aleta somehow made it through the last room.

He looked around, scoping out the concrete bunker-like perimeter behind the press of bodies. It had the appearance of having been well-used, and most of the rubble had been cleared. There was a small shaft off to one side that might once have housed a service elevator. It would hopefully allow him to escape out of there, if he could matter-transfer back to the Eye and scoot up into it in time. But Jordyn had no idea where it went except away from Aleta, and he was determined not to leave her behind. Plus, he wanted to stay long enough to at least meet and identify the other celestial entity.

Many of the feral beings surrounding him were typical of the demonic creations of Baal, but some were clearly human and demon crossed hybrids, something he had feared happening. They made no attempt to swarm him or do more than just block his way even though most were armed with gruesome looking weapons. There were far too many of them to hope to do much damage in a preemptive attack, and the rest would just swarm in and pull him down. Unless he let go of his corporeal form and disappeared into the Eye first for regeneration, his mortal body could die from wounds, and then he'd go back to being bodiless somewhere remote out in space. It would take far too long to gather the strength to come back to Earth, which would not do the almost decimated human race any good.

"Great gods, you're an ugly and ragtag bunch of cowards! What in all the heavens are you waiting for—an invitation?" He spoke to them in their own language, putting on a show of bravado. If Jordyn was going to sacrifice himself, he wanted to take out their ascended leader at the same time, and could think of no better way of drawing that being forth than insulting the followers.

"They're waiting for *me*," said a rough and guttural voice from the other side of the room, and the host parted like waves as a scythe was hoisted over it. A dark armor-clad male figure strode confidently between them, coming forward to face Jordyn in the center of the arena. He bore the mark of the angelic legion on his brow, and his quietly commanding tone had the seraphic level of vibrating resonance.

"My, aren't you the ugly one, and quite full of yourself too," Jordyn said evenly, to prove he was less than impressed.

Eyes glowing sickly yellow, his thickly matted war braids rustled as the dark angel shook his shaggy head in negative disbelief. A malicious smile played about thin lips over a salt and pepper straggling beard stained ruddy. He studied the slender, somewhat wavering, androgynous figure standing before him dressed in tightly fitted dark clothing accented with white lace, half the blonde hair stiffly vertical and the other half falling light and loose about the shoulders. This challenger's bright aquamarine eyes were circled darkly with kohl, which meant he too was having trouble dealing with the yellow sun that lurked behind the roiling clouds, but most importantly, *there was no weapon in hand.*

The dark one holding the scythe threw back his head and began to laugh, a harsh and maniacal sound.

"I fail to see what is so incredibly humorous about all this," Jordyn said in a disarming way with gloved hands on his slim hips and an arched eyebrow raised.

The dark being sighed. "It's you I find so entertaining, pathetic thing that you are. I was expecting at least a reasonably potent challenger to represent the mortals, and what do they conjure up? The court jester! Humans never fail to amuse and disappoint me."

"Things are not always as simple as they appear," the celestial hunter of lost souls said lightly as he began to pace back and forth just a bit, shuffling his boots in the dust. "For one thing, what makes you think the humans called me? Maybe I was just hanging around this part of their universe and decided to come down and have a look-see. I'm sure I'm far from the only bored has-been spook in the neighborhood, now that the big guns have all gone off to conquer new territory."

That was a bit of a prick under the thin skin of his very dangerous opponent, and Jordyn did it on purpose. He was already sizing up this would-be new leader of the damned as an egotistical, overbearing sociopath. Jordyn knew that some traits didn't disappear simply because a soul ascended, especially if that entity was given a title and some manner of wielding power over those underneath. As the ascended being became more corporeal again, the most marked of the original personality quirks would tend to resurface. Already this one was agitated at being tweaked, and while he was doubtless very powerful and dangerous, that temper made him somewhat more likely to slip up and do or say something that would lead to his downfall. The calculating mind of the last scion of House Orion was as sharp as his tongue.

"Do you have any idea who you're dealing with, little clown?" the dark angel said with venom, and his eyes nearly threw sparks as his anger grew and he began to slowly circle Jordyn with a predatory attitude.

"Of course I do," Jordyn said lightly, but his eyes went just as hard as his opponent's as he took a defensive posture. He waved his hands around overhead, wiggling his fingers like a conjurer. "You're the big bad bogeyman! And I'm supposed to be oh, so frightened of you!" he added, clasping his hands over his heart quite dramatically. He made all kinds of melodramatic faces and gestures, mocking the other ascended being, who was now glaring at him with anger and hatred so palpable it could be sensed in the room. Even some of the undead gasped at Jordyn's purposely flippant attitude.

"I should just kill you now for your arrogance," the dark one said, and then he swept the scythe down suddenly. It blurred through the air, faster than any mortal eye could track it.

Jordyn had been expecting that, and timed his leap. He cleared it with inches to spare. "Missed me!" he said brightly, and smiled with wicked glee. He had felt the arc of power coming long before the blade began to drop. This one was missing some of the electrifying dynamism that marked his class of entity, and that too should work in Jordyn's favor. "You're terribly slow you know," he said sidestepping another vicious chop by darting sideways, and then vaulted overhead to land on the other side of the dark angel. "You'll have to do better than that," Jordyn added, pressing him.

"Don't toy with me unless you want to suddenly wind up in Limbo with no way out this time," the furious entity warned him. He was clearly agitated that Jordyn had been able to evade his killing cuts.

"Oh I'm sure you could very easily order that too," Jordyn said in a more serious voice as he continued to hopscotch back and forth before him. "*If you still had the power to do so, that is.*"

The wielded scythe crossing in and out of the spirit world was a dead giveaway now; this was one of the Four Horsemen of the Apocalypse come back again. It was commonly known that those fallen angels had been stripped of their power over immortals, and so could no longer ordain the end of anything above a human gone astray.

"I have killed far better than you with just a glance," Jordyn's opponent warned, as he began to spin the scythe back and forth, and around at a dizzying pace that was hard to follow, in preparation for a flurry of slicing and chopping attacks.

"So I've heard," Jordyn said dryly as he began to back off a bit. "Samael then, I presume?" he said with an inclination of his head that showed a bit of deference, as that was the heavenly name of one of the lower angelic beings who was destined to be present at any of the ends of mortal time. Samael's purpose was supposed to be limited to guiding the unclaimed souls of the nonbeliever dead onward toward oblivion, and definitely not to make more of them. The current godless state of Earth must have drawn him like a magnet, and then his overblown ego supplied the rest of the incentive to improvise.

Samael nodded, and he smiled in a way that was not at all pleasant. "Very good for a fool, you've guessed correctly. But tell me… what is this nonsense about? A single weak-powered imbecile from the House of Orion has come to challenge me? You're the best humankind can summon to their aid?" He laughed and so did his gathered host, a hideous sound, as it came from cruel and gruesome faces, most of them not much more than grinning misshapen skulls stretched with scabrous skin and baring sharp, unaligned teeth. "You're hardly worth bothering with."

"Well then, you can just let me go I suppose," Jordyn said in an airy way, as they began to circle one another in earnest this time, the death lord with his great scythe, and the hunter of lost souls with the only weapon he had—his wits. Jordyn had noticed right away when he was able to outrun Samael that there was a reason the dark angel had not registered fully on his senses: Samael had given up some of his ability to dissipate energy and teleport. That was likely a trade-off to become fully corporeal, which gave him the ability to inflict physical damage. So he was already caught up in causing his own part of the carnage that would bring humanity to its knees. That knowledge might actually work in Jordyn's favor if he continued to be quick enough to keep avoiding being split asunder, and then some other situation intervened.

"I hope you're prepared to be sent back to the Essence Level forever this time," Samael said with a sneer as he made a few more arm-crossing, back and forth feints with the scythe, which lithe and agile Jordyn nimbly leaped over, past, or sidestepped. Samael's ploy was to take the center of the floor and not move around as much as simply pivot, keeping his quite energetic foe continually dancing on his toes until he tired out, when he as the slower but more powerful adversary would move in for the kill.

Flashing about like quicksilver, Jordyn knew that if he was reading the situation correctly, Samael wanted to eliminate him all by himself, making an example to his followers that their leader was virtually invincible. That impression would be doubly important down the road, for as they spread, the undead host would be called upon to face even stronger members of the Divine Class than the latest heir of House Orion.

It was a single-minded attitude that might also prove his downfall. Accordingly, Samael's well-indoctrinated subordinates would not intervene in this battle between godlings unless their leader was mortally threatened, and Jordyn wanted to make sure they were fearful enough of him to make even that unlikely. It would be best to play to Samael's ego as well, and make it look as if he himself was similarly overconfident and oblivious to the overall implications of the dark angel's toying with him. If there was one thing Jordyn Orion excelled at, it was deceit, for many of the trickster deities of the out-worlds had been of his line.

"Nice little place you have here," Jordyn said, pulling the Eye of Providence from his shirt and letting it light up the interior, blinding most of the undead momentarily and the lesser ones permanently. Before he could absorb into it, Samael's scythe swept down and tried to take his hand off, and then he came back at Jordyn with the butt end of the handle. He succeeded in knocking the Eye to the floor, where it rolled away, sending sparkles of energy out around it.

One of the demons, another tall one with curling ram's horns and an almost human expression, bent to pick it up. The trap was set and about to be sprung.

"Don't touch that thing you fool!" Samael yelled out too late, for as soon as the skeletal fingers clasped the orb; it radiated energy that made the creature's entire body quake. The demon reared back with a howl of agony as it began to crackle and split apart and light rays emanated from inside it. The body arched and recoiled in its death throes, bumping into several of his brethren before he suddenly erupted into an explosion of dusty shards

...pulling the Eye of Providence from his shirt...

and nova-like emissions. The chain reaction took out four or five more of the nearest bestial things, turning them into vaporizing fragments for just having contact with the one who had touched the source energy. The rest scrambled away from them. The dazzling, scalding light that had been released in that demon's passing blinded a few more.

"Naughty, naughty to try and steal my essence," Jordyn said with a cackle and a little skipping victory dance as he alternately waggled and pointed both forefingers at the now crumpled piles of grave dust with a couple jagged homemade swords and an axe laying across them. He smirked at Samael. "I suspect that must have drained you just a little too, or otherwise you would have taken another swipe at me. The light of truth hurts, doesn't it?"

Samael's rage and frustration caused him to momentarily flicker, and Jordyn had expected that reaction, for the death angel and his demons were linked negative energy, and Jordyn's vibration was definitely positive. The Eye was powerful, and as long as he knew where it was, it was safe. Jordyn always knew where the Eye was, for it was part of him, and he was part of it. And he also knew that a good portion of the Samael's power came from his adoring worshipers, so any loss was going to affect the Angel of Death as well.

Samael's blinded minions were moaning and digging at their suddenly useless eyes and their fear and loss of faith was starting to stagger him. There had been another large passing of their kind into oblivion that they could now sense, and many of them were now becoming uncertain enough of the outcome that they began to withdraw.

To remind them of who was still in charge, Samael thrust out his arms, still tightly gripping his mostly symbolic but still quite sharp scythe; making a show of being unconcerned. "My family and I welcome you to our new and spacious home." The area went Stygian dark, the Eye the only bright point in there. "Too bad you won't be staying with us long."

There was an awed muttering from all around Jordyn, as some of the blinded ones had regained at least a bit of sight with the sudden onset of almost total darkness again. And so most lingered, waiting...

Jordyn knew that Samael meant he was claiming the entire world and not just the basements of the bombed out city that they were standing in. Unsmiling, he drew a bit of energy off the Eye, lighting up his face for the others as he pointed at Samael and frowned under lowered brows, his visage growing increasingly harsher in the contrast between dark and light.

"This is far from *your* home Samael. You know the rules of occupation, once we renounce the material plane, we are supposed to move on after our assignment is done. You and your pets have no place here and as always in the past, they will die off and you will become powerless again."

That got them good and agitated. Each new batch of demonic creations thought they were the first to ever be brought to life.

"And exactly who is left to enforce this?" Samael asked lightly. "You?" He smirked, but his eyes had the look of a cornered animal—*dangerous*. To confront him with the rules of cosmic order in front of his loyal horde was more than a challenge; it was an insult as well as a ploy to usurp his hold over them by sowing more doubt in their rather simple minds. They both knew that meant the gauntlet was down.

"Yes, me!" Jordyn said, digging a thumb into his chest in his vehemence. "Me, myself, and I, actually. It's exactly why I felt compelled to come here."

"He felt...*compelled*...to come and tell me how to run my new world. Isn't that interesting?" Samael said with a snarl. "I'm through with this foolishness Orion; your line ends here and now."

He began fighting in earnest, whirling and whipping the scythe up and down, around and back with blinding speed, relentlessly pressing Jordyn toward the snapping maws of his bestial companions. But Jordyn had well sown the seeds of self-preservation amongst them, for they backed away instead of supporting their leader, afraid to touch the Starman and be exploded like the one who had taken up his orb.

As he continually danced and vaulted out of harm's way, Jordyn called to the Eye, but Samael saw it moving. The scythe batted it away, into the undead host. It landed at the feet of one of the larger ones, who backpedaled and shoved his peers out of the way to get farther from it. Their fear of Jordyn and his glowing ball of destruction was enough that they were not going to be much help, and so it should at least come down to a one-on-one battle, which was far more fair, though Jordyn knew Samael was most likely to win in the end.

I just hope Aleta got through her part of this alive! Jordyn prayed to who or whatever might care as he dodged and weaved around the arena with the scythe slashing and hacking all around him, the fanatical single-minded determination of his adversary keeping him constantly on the move. He couldn't keep up that kind of pace forever, but was desperately waiting for an opening to take the Grim Reaper back to oblivion with him.

~

Aleta slumped, exhausted and gasping, in the middle of a room coated black with the soot of the raging flames that had spouted from her body not moments before. Not so much as a spider or a cockroach survived, for all living things in that fiery tomb had been incinerated to ashes and coals. Every single demon in there perished, many of them screeching in agony as their bodies burned up before they could scramble up the walls or tug down the solid material blocking the doors. Once she had calmed down, there were no secondary flames as most of the truly combustible things had burned off long ago with the bombing and flash fires, and what had been left had been scavenged by the early survivors as fuel during the long nuclear winters. Any fire left after the demons were gone quickly snuffed out.

She took a few staggering steps forward to where the door should be, and almost tripped over a smoking skeleton. "I need light," she said, holding out a palm. It took a couple of minutes of intense concentration, because she was so physically drained and emotionally exhausted, but eventually a small wavering flame ignited. It was enough to see where she was going.

Holding the flame in one palm before her, Aleta stumbled over to the blocked opening where Jordyn had disappeared, and touched the metal with the unoccupied hand. It was still hot, and thick enough not to have been distorted in the blaze, so she could not move it. Leaning in, unfazed by the heat of it, she could hear faint sounds issued from the other side— screeches and voices raised, some of which sounded like more of the creatures she had just defeated.

"I have to go to him. If he's still alive, he needs my help," she said tiredly, her throat raw with the dryness of yelling while having channeled flame throughout her body. Enough of the adrenaline rush of the battle was left to propel her back out to study the room, especially the parts of the walls where the creatures had climbed. Aleta had often clambered into the trees and vines of the forested part of her home land, and she was lightweight and agile enough to attempt to make it to the ceiling level of the basement she was in. The demonic crawlers had continued to swarm inside even after the openings were blocked, and so there had to be other ways out.

She couldn't climb with the flame in her palm though, but needed it to see what she was doing. Aleta stood perplexed a few moments and then placed the flame on top of her head, freeing up both hands for climbing. She carefully made her way up a wall and then to the ceiling level, inching slowly along over half melted pipes and glowing iron beams toward the top of the metallic barrier that divided the room she was in from where she hoped to find Jordyn Orion.

Oh please let him still be alive, she prayed. *If the gods favor me in any way, don't take Jordyn from me, he's the only hope I have left of getting out of this cursed land!*

~

Samael had grown tired of the cat-and-mouse game with Jordyn and so after a couple more vicious sweeps that almost got the Starman but didn't, he called a halt to it.

"Giving up already?" Jordyn asked brightly, trying very hard to hide his exhaustion. He was grateful for the break.

"No… I'm just hungry," Samael retorted, for he was about to try another tactic. "Abbadon," he barked, and the demon warily slunk to his side.

"Yes Master?" he replied, never taking his hate-filled eyes off Jordyn, who had by the magic of the Holy Starlight, managed to kill his eldest son.

"Bring me something tender to eat. And bring it *alive*. I want the pleasure of dining before Master Orion."

"Very good Master," the creature said with a bow and a triumphant smirk at Jordyn before it disappeared.

Jordyn watched coolly the entire time, not willing to show any emotions, not even for the innocent life he was not going to be able to protect. After sparring with Samael and realizing they were fairly evenly matched, he had a plan, but it would take near perfect timing, and whatever poor human they brought back to sacrifice in order to bend his will was not going to survive it.

I hope I have a chance to explain why this had to be to its spirit when we get on the other side!

"Why do you hate humans so much?" he asked Samael quietly in Old High Angelic as they waited for the demon to drag in whatever captive they were going to try and make him beg mercy for.

"Because they are piteously contemptible fools who die far too easily, yet are arrogant enough to think they can outwit death by praying for salvation," was the answer he got. As he spoke there was a chorus of wailing in the background behind the Angel of Death, and the sound of padding feet getting closer.

"Most of them do get over that in the end," Jordyn commented but couldn't keep the dread from his voice this time. The crying sounded very young…

"Perhaps. But ah, now there's a lovely sight for you," Samael said in a chortling tone as the company behind him parted and Abbadon stalked back into view. The demon stepped forward dragging his captive before Jordyn, whose spirit sank at the sight.

Abbadon held the arms of a terrified little girl of maybe three years old. Just old enough to be cognizant of what was going on; she sobbed and gibbered in pain and terror.

She had been a pretty little thing that followed Aleta everywhere, watching the slender, dark-skinned woman with big, round pale eyes and a thumb stuck in her mouth. Now her short brown hair was matted and filthy, and her disheveled clothing was torn and spattered with the spray of arterial blood from her mother's dying attempts at trying to defend her only living child to the last of her strength. The little girl's torso was covered in claw marks and festering sores from being manhandled, and one of her little shoulders appeared to be dislocated. She dangled helplessly in the arms of the creature of nightmares, her eyes rolling in shock and purely subconscious awareness of vile cruelties that no human child should ever have to see or experience. Her will to live had already died and as the demon laid her out on the arena floor, her body was about to follow.

"You don't have to do this," Jordyn said quietly. "She's just one little life Samael; meaningless to you when you consider how many more are out there waiting for you to tell them what their master wants from them." He was stalling for time, hoping that something his prickling senses could feel, a subtle change in the climate of the room, was more than just wishful thinking.

"Oh, but I do!" Samael said with malicious delight, as he watched the play of emotions in the aquamarine eyes of the heir of Orion. There would be no bargaining or running away now, because he knew Jordyn Orion to be an oath-bound human helper, and he would stay to protect the innocent soul that was about to be released to oblivion. "She's important to me because her death is going to mean something very damning to you, since it's your fault!"

He raised the scythe just as Jordyn made up his mind what was most important of all, sparing the little tot the pain of being gutted and tortured while still alive enough to realize what was happening, or sacrificing his own plans to civilize Earth by taking out the death angel now and stopping this madness. Either way, the little girl was as good as dead.

May your soul forgive me, little one, but there are so few of you left and far too many out there like these monsters! Jordyn's muscles tensed while his mind was stuck somewhere between grief and fury. He sent the summons that began pulling the Eye of Providence surreptitiously his way. This was going to end now!

"You've been such an engaging guest, I'm going to give you the first taste," Samael said with glee as the scythe swooped down.

And that was when something behind Jordyn exploded, and one end of the room became filled with flames!

~

Aleta had laboriously crawled over everything in her path toward a distant dim light that shone through a small opening above the wall of metal that had blocked the doorway. There was not much room to spare, just a crawlspace big enough to squeeze into. She would have missed it, if not for a sudden flare of brilliant white light that accompanied some loud screeches. The far end lit up again for a couple of minutes as she made her laborious way slowly toward that opening and wriggled inside, worming along determinedly on elbows and knees, pushing with her feet and dragging with hands until she got to where she could peer out and view the assembly below.

She was just in time to see the small child brought in, and realized what was about to happen. Thankful beyond belief that at least Jordyn was still alive, she gradually twisted herself around like a boneless cat in that small area, and then, feet first, prepared for the long drop down into the room beyond.

That child is someone's daughter. She could be my sister. That makes her one of my own kin. She does not deserve to die like this! Aleta stoked her emotions until she felt the heat rising in her blood and spreading through her body as she pushed out of the opening and began the almost one story drop to the floor, shouting and beginning to flare up on the way down.

Many dark eyes looked up and were instantly burned out as the glaring light and searing heat of the yellow sun of their ancestors came belching down on them. Aleta landed flaming hot and flaring outward on top of a milling pileup of tightly packed demon bodies which shifted and heaved beneath her, unearthly death screams of panic turning to agony as they caught fire and began to burn. A few stalwart and foolhardy ones of the elite guard tried to rush in and bludgeon her, but soon found themselves afire or with weapons too hot to hold onto as she swirled and blew flames all over them. Her fire could not explode them as Jordyn's star energy could, but it burned through them easily enough, and she was about to set that entire room alight.

As the scythe had come down for its first cut, the small child had closed her eyes and died of fright rather than suffer any further pain or indignity at the hands of her captors. His concentration broken at that critical moment, Samael had not been able to claim her life fast enough. The Angel of Death knew it immediately, and he howled in frustration as he was cheated in the end by a tiny defiant spirit who had chosen her own time to vacate her now lifeless body. The little one lay serene and untouched before him as his energy flickered and withdrew, unable to deal with the sudden losses atop his victim's uncooperative demise. And now flaming death stalked his minions, and that threatened him as well.

As Jordyn Orion lunged at him, Samael broke away and ran for the nearest exit.

"Get out of my way Jordyn!" Aleta snarled, her blazing eyes set on a gradually disappearing Samael, which even she recognized as the ringleader. "I'm about to cook myself something quite foul." Trailing flames behind her, she spread her arms wide and advanced on the Angel of Death, who was torn between taking a stand and making a hasty retreat. He chose the later, whatever was left of his demonic forces scrambling quickly after him as roaring, crackling flames began to fill the room.

"You do what you need to, I have other business to attend," a jubilantly relieved Jordyn Orion said as he scooped up the limp and cooling, but still intact body of a very brave little girl, and then summoned the now brightly glowing orb to hand. "I will find you later Aleta, good hunting!" He disappeared into the Eye of Providence with the dead girl in his arms, and just managed to make it up the old shaft and out of range as a surge of heat worthy of a solar flare erupted into that room, killing any and all beings not fast enough to exit. As for those who did, a furious and vengeful guardian spirit of fire followed them through the entire underground complex, completely burning out every area she could get into.

Most of the Children of Baal that lived in that area died that day, their wizened flesh burned off, their blackened and twisted bones lying in crumbled heaps where they fell. None dared turn and face the fiery wrath of the elemental being as she relentlessly harried and stalked them. In the end only a few survived, and they turned tail and abandoned an exhausted, greatly weakened, yet still defiant Samael when she caught up with him at last.

They faced off against one another in a place where he had never expected to make his last stand, the very center of what had been his small universe; the bombed out apse of the old cathedral. He stood wavering and shaky, holding onto his scythe for support, greatly reduced in power now that most of his supporters had been killed off.

"You can't actually kill me witch," he told her as she advanced on him a step at a time, flames flaring all around her body as she backed him up against what was left of the wall where once a great crucifix had hung, the symbol of the faith whose laws he was supposed to uphold. "I'm immortal after all."

"No but I can cleanse your soul for you," she said with malice dripping like venom in every word. "Welcome to Hell, oath breaker!" And with that Aleta summoned every ounce of strength she had left. Bringing her hands together before her while blowing out as hard as she could, she deliberately directed all her fire energy forward and watched dispassionately as it engulfed him. Samael never cried aloud, but his mouth opened in a silent rictus of agony, as his clothing burned off and his mortal flesh slumped away, baring his bones. In the end there was nothing left but the skeletal ghost of what was once the mighty Angel of Death, now just a grim reaper of souls again. It flickered and then went dim, disappearing in a light puff of smoke that a wailing wind blew away.

Aleta Kalama was exhausted, and her flame went out. She fell to her knees, and then went prostrate, her fire spent and her insensate body vulnerable to anything or anyone that should come upon her.

A Dedicated Life

When Jordyn Orion in his spiritual essence came out of that shaft, he was outside what had once been a great towering building where people had made foolish decisions about trade and monetary matters—decisions that had lead up to the war that had ultimately wiped most of them out. Still in essence mode, he allowed a wind that had sprung up to drift him away from the city, noting with satisfaction that fires were springing up all over as Aleta hunted down her quarry. A few ragged, staggering humans had escaped captivity and were running back toward the settlement, using clubs, torches, or whatever else they could find to take on any of the half-blinded undead they came across. They would inform their peers of all they had seen, and just exactly who and what had come to save them.

Flaming Aleta, in mastering her own fears, had kindled the fight to live free again back into the hearts of those people.

Jordyn drifted away to a nearby hillock where the wind seemed to be coming from, for he had felt a compelling summons and it was one who was not to be ignored.

She was standing there waiting for him, the tall and unsmiling phantom warrior queen of old. Her dark shroud of crow, raven and vulture feathers was draped over her shoulders, her long, sleek black hair arrayed over it, face and arms tattooed with warrior symbols, sword sheathed at her side. She turned her dark and unreadable eyes toward the city below as it burned, and smiled without mirth. The Morrigan loved a good battle.

Jordyn Orion left his essence, and became mortal again some distance off as a sign of deference for the war deity on the hill, who far outranked him. He squatted down and picked up the orb, tucking it inside his shirt and with the dead girl child in his arms, walked slowly up the hill toward the tall, dark goddess with his head bowed and his senses on alert. The Morrigan was not known for being overly friendly or cooperative. He stopped a short distance from the top and waited to be addressed.

When she did speak, her voice was deep and resonant. "Well met, Son of Orion, I see you've found yourself a fire elemental with some fight in her. Brighid is somewhere around here as well. I think she will be jealous that she did not claim that one first." She turned to look at him, and Jordyn had trouble meeting her eyes, they were so intense in their searching glare. She seemed amused at that. Looking down at the small, dead body cradled in his arms, she sighed. "I feel Samael's foul spirit is leaving us. Too late to save this one I see."

"She chose her own time once again," he said simply. "Her spirit left to avoid becoming Samael's next sacrificial meal and increasing his hold on the Children of Baal."

The Morrigan seemed intrigued as she studied the girl's scratched and battered face, so very peaceful in death. "Quite interesting that she was so young with that much resistance in her. Yet hers is an old soul, and in this incarnation, she has been baptized in her mother's battle blood. She no longer serves the Yahweh, for He has moved on with his Chosen, so now I can claim her as my own."

The tall, dark haired goddess put out her tattooed and muscular arms and Jordyn stepped forward and laid the body of the toddler in them. She drew the girl in toward her, and held her reverently. "This one is near to my heart, for she is a natural fighter. I will see that she is reborn to hunt the Children of Baal in our next time of need. Many thanks for all your help."

"Her name was Joan, and she was a refugee child who came to this city with her mother," Jordyn said simply. "She's Joan of Orleans, I was told. I hated to see her die this way–"

"I know who she was, and what they did to her in the past. Yet this time she is mine to train, and I do not make martyrs without a good reason. Things will be different."

The Morrigan turned with a flourish of her feathered cloak and spoke not another word before she simply vanished. Jordyn bowed his head in respect before he walked away, and with the help of the Eye, teleported back down to the city to find Aleta, and tell her what an amazing woman she really was.

~

Soft footfalls fell behind Aleta, it was the sound of someone slipping up. Likely one of the few remaining demons, though it was still daylight and most of them could not handle the light. She wanted to arise and meet this new threat, but couldn't find the strength to do more than groan and flop over.

The light behind her was blinding, almost as fiery as her own flames, but seen from the outside, she knew it had nothing to do with her own abilities. Aleta now had somewhat of an idea how she appeared to others. Within a pillar of steady blaze that burned without heat or crackling noises was the figure of a woman of medium height and build. She studied Aleta and smiled, and then waved her arms until the flames died down, before she stepped forward.

"Arise, Daughter of Fire," she said in a light, sweet voice that had a slight echo and a lilting cadence to it, and made a lifting motion with her hands. Aleta found herself standing before a pale-skinned woman with a freckled face and arms, her long red hair held back in a shining gold circlet with a flame motif, and very piercing green eyes. She was dressed in white and gold robes. At her feet were a harp and a forge, in her hands, she cradled a small flame. "I am well pleased with you today," she continued, her voice seeming like it came from afar.

"Who...are you?" Aleta inquired quietly, tired and confused. She had never seen this woman in the settlement before and yet there was something about her that was familiar, though it also seemed that she did not really belong to their world. She reminded Aleta of Jordyn, and her heart ached to see him.

The woman smiled. "I am called many things by many people, but most commonly Brighid. I am the keeper of the Sacred Flame that lights mankind's darkest hours. I would be your patroness, if you will dedicate to me, and fight for your people, Aleta Kalama."

"Wait—you know my name?" Aleta said with suspicion.

Brighid nodded, and her little flame guttered just a bit, "I know much about you, Aleta, enough that I would choose you as one of my flame keepers. I do not think Jordyn Orion would mind that overly much," she said with a smile.

"Of course not. Jordyn Orion would never think to interfere in the affairs of the High Divine," said a very welcome and familiar voice from somewhere behind Aleta, and she turned joyously to embrace her companion. "I will stand aside and let Aleta decide for herself, but I would like to tell her that I approve, if that is acceptable to you, Lady Brighid." He eyed the goddess roguishly, as she was one of his favorites amongst the divine.

"It is, but you already have told her, Jordyn, as you full well know," Brighid said with a sigh. Turning back to Aleta, she said, "If you accept my patronage child, take from me this flame as a token of our bond. Wear it always, and know that I am with you wherever you walk."

Aleta paused a moment, looking first at Brighid, and then at Jordyn, who lifted an eyebrow and shrugged. It was her decision then.

"My life has changed so much that I guess, well, why not?" Aleta reached out for the flame. It was cold and did not burn her hands, but immediately extinguished, leaving a small silver pendant on a length of fine chain, the likes of which had not been seen on Earth for hundreds of years. "Thank you," Aleta said with feeling but when she looked up, the goddess was already gone and she was saddened. Her shoulders slumped and a single tear slid out of her left eye, to run down her cheek.

"Let me help you put that on," Jordyn told her, and he pushed her hair out of the way as she brought the chain to her neck. The pendant had an open pentacle star design in finely worked silver with a golden flame backdrop.

"Does this mean something important?" Aleta said, looking down to where it lay against her rich brown skin.

"It means you are now the first member of an elite group," Jordyn said in the most serious voice she had ever heard him use, and he pulled a very similar chain from his own shirt. It held a silver pentacle pendant, something Aleta had never noticed before, but his had a backdrop with all sorts of symbols and colors that seemed to shift and change as she looked at them. Only the silver pentagram symbol stayed constant.

"I'm glad we're doing whatever it is we're supposed to do, together," Aleta said as they made their way out of the old cathedral and back through the city into the dusk toward the settlement once more.

"I am too," Jordyn said simply, and for once, he sounded very, very sincere.

WHERE FAIR WINDS DO BLOW

Aboard The Curlew

Aleta Kalama had never traveled on water before. She found the rolling feeling and the action of the waves disconcerting at first. The brief trip in the small rowboat that took them out to the bigger ship anchored in the bay wasn't too bad, though being so close to such deep water was frightening, for she had never learned how to swim. As they grew close to the larger vessel though, she was overwhelmed with fear. That was when it really sank in that she was leaving dry land behind, albeit for a short journey on their first hop.

At least that's what Jordyn had told her, maybe a day and a night for this initial voyage. Aleta had never traveled anywhere that her own two feet couldn't take her. Looking down at the choppy water, and then up toward the low boat with the tall mast, it made her feel very uneasy in the pit of her stomach. At the very thought of bobbing around on the water, the small, lightly boned woman with the rich brown skin and lustrous dark hair perspired so profusely that even her unnaturally high body temperature could not burn it all off. Between that and the amount of salty spray in the air, her clothing stuck damply to her lithe form.

Jordyn Orion sat next to her on the plank seat, fidgeting while eagerly scanning the water ahead as the smaller boat's several pairs of oars dipped and rolled in unison. As far as he could recall, he had never traveled on water before either. After hurtling through space and time as an energy being, the feeling of the boat was similar, though a lot more tactile. He found that his still relatively new corporeal human form was a plethora of such sensations, and the excitement of each additional discovery was wondrous. His head swiveled back and forth, reveling in every new sight and sound, and even the persistent mist against his very pale skin didn't bother him. His very bright aquamarine eyes, circled with dark kohl against the glare of whatever part of Earth's yellow sunlight poked through the clouds, darted here and there, taking in everything they could—cataloging this, memorizing that...

These shallow, flat bottomed boats that could reach the shoreline only operated in the daytime, which was their way of keeping any of what the true humans termed 'defectives'—mutated cannibalistic humanoids raised from the dead—from spreading to other lands across the water. Jordyn and Aleta understood better than most why that prohibition was so important, for they had just dealt with a group of those beings that he referred to as the Children of Baal, named for an old world god who had created the first generation of them back in Earth's prehistory. It was the grateful munificence of the relieved populace of the nearby settlement, as well as the cooperation of the remnants of the local naval forces, that earned them their passage aboard the ocean voyaging boat they were ultimately berthed upon.

The crew, a taciturn quartet, bent to the task, either not comprehending the blathering of the two new passengers aboard or not caring what they said. Jordyn could understand them easily though. With the help of the Eye of Providence, the orb of his celestial essence, Jordyn Orion, The Hunter of Lost Souls, could translate or speak just about any language. His eyes took in everything, including the construction of the ship they were rapidly approaching and the condition of the sea around them as he listened to the crewmen talk of having dealt with such challenges as kraken, sea serpents, and tribute to demanding merfolk while on the longer voyages. Since those were deemed the creatures of old myths and tales, either they were all daft liars, or the space/time continuum was seriously fractured and Earth's past, as well as parts of other dimensions, were leaking through. He had suspected that anyway, but time would tell, and he was not about to share his revelations with an already apprehensive Aleta.

"Are you sure there's no way by land to wherever we are going?" she asked him with trepidation in her voice, as the bigger boat loomed closer still. They could make out its lengthwise arched planking now.

"No there isn't, but I wouldn't be so uneasy Aleta," Jordan said, squeezing her trembling hand as they drew alongside. "I'm positive it's quite safe, and the weather looks absolutely brilliant for a fast trip."

"So you keep saying," she retorted uneasily as they began to edge in toward the boarding area.

The boat they were taking to the next coast was a long, low draft thing of composite material that had been bent and formed into well tarred overlapping planks. The sail was a single large sheet, made from some sort of fiber woven tight and painted with a pair of watchful eyes. Jordyn knew that the effect was very reminiscent of an ancient Viking longship on a smaller scale. The prow curved up similarly into a fanciful replica of a sea serpent head. There were other people on board, but they mostly looked like crew.

The rowboat was snugged alongside and a knotted rope was tossed over. They would have to use that to hoist themselves in, and then the crew would hand up what little baggage they had along with the rest of the cargo, before shoving off again. The last ship-to-shore run of the day for the rowboats let off any passengers or crew that wished to be on land. When the smaller boats where not in use, they were anchored in the bay or tied to pilings well out in the water, where no beings unable to swim could reach them. It was an awkward system, but had become the only safe way to run a naval fleet and not allow access to genetically dangerous stowaways that would endanger their other ports of call.

After Aleta and Jordyn were aboard, their punched metal tickets were checked and then an extra embossing was added to each before they were allowed to hang them back around their necks on the woven lanyards they had been issued. After they were processed, the tall, sandy haired, middle-aged captain, in her parka and boots, stepped forward and laid out the rules. They were the only passengers on this voyage, so she addressed them directly.

"My name is Hulda. Welcome aboard the Curlew. This is a very stable vessel, and quite a fast one, so I hope you will be pleased with the ride. We will be traveling by the wind, which is why we're under a bare pole now. If you hold up a hand, you will see the blow is toward the northeast, which is very much in the direction we'll be headed. When we get to the Unified Islands, we'll drop you at a docking area out a'sea, and a ferry will take you and your belongings to the Solstice, which is a kite ship with a thorium drive system. The Solstice is a cargo vessel, so t'will not be as luxurious as some of the passenger frigates, but you are lucky to be gaining a berth on it at all. Please be prepared for some inconveniences. Open water travel is tricky these days, and I want you to keep that in mind and do as the captain and crew asks of you. Now, are there any questions?"

Jordyn and Aleta looked at one another. What was there to say?

"Very good then. Enjoy your trip." The captain went to her station at the fore and the rudder man went aft. Jordyn and Aleta went under the canopy that covered the deck behind the oarsmen, and took seats on boxes and barrels amongst the now roped together cargo. When the last rowboat was unloaded and made fast to a piling, with the crew all aboard, the sail was unfurled and tied fast as it snapped taut, catching the wind.

It bellied and filled. Slowly at first, but then gaining speed, the ship slipped away from the sight of land and into the waves, cresting some and diving into others. The Curlew was strake-built on the length, to be able to twist and curve with the movement of the water, and skimmed the surface more than cut through it. Jordyn considered it great fun, and laughed and clapped at each rise and fall. But Aleta was soon seasick and miserable. She often had to lean over the side with her hands on the gunwales, heaving her guts out.

"I will never get used to this!" she moaned miserably, wiping her mouth with the back of one hand.

"Oh, I'm sure you will adjust in time," Jordyn said, patting her back as she retched and gagged some more.

The captain gave someone else her watch and came aft, squatting beside Jordyn and Aleta, her blue eyes showing concern. "This is the first time a'sea for her I take it?" she said to Jordyn. He nodded and cringed away, trying not to let mist-borne vomit fly into his carefully teased blonde hair.

"She's going to be worse on the container ship if you hit rough water because they tend to roll more than slide through waves like this. I'll make sure she gets some pressure bands and a supply of datura patches, and you can ask their cookie about ginger tea—they'll have at least a limited supply if you're lucky. Stay on deck as much as the weather allows and amidships if possible. Sorry that you're having such a rough time," she added, and easily rising to her feet, walked back to the fore part of the ship again.

"I like her," Aleta said weakly, once she had exhausted most of what her stomach could churn up again.

"I do too," Jordyn said warmly, and planned on keeping Hulda in mind if he ever needed small vessel access to a nearby area. A boat like the Curlew could easily work its way up an estuary, and it was light enough that a party of strong people could portage it. With care, it might even make it across the big water, though with some of the seasoned sailors' stories he had been hearing, he doubted that would be deemed practical.

Aleta was tired and laid down. Wrapped up in her cloak, she curled up across a couple of boxes, eventually falling into a light and troubled sleep. Jordyn sat watching her for a bit, thinking about how they were going to need warmer wear for when they were on the ocean proper, and then his thoughts wandered to what the next part of their journey together might bring. Once they made the crossing and reached the still somewhat green continent everyone referred to as Columbiana, he was going to start searching in earnest for the other elemental beings he had come to find. He wasn't sure what was pulling him there, but an Orion learned early to never ignore the nagging of that inner voice, and his was telling him to go. And of course, dear Aleta had to come with him, for she was just learning to use her abilities to produce and control fire.

As the sun that they could not quite see set on the western horizon, which at that point was nothing but open water, Jordyn snuggled up to Aleta and put his arm around her, marveling at her warmth. She smiled in her sleep, hiccuped and belched a few times, and then rolled into him, tucking her small dark haired head under his jutting chin, before she blissfully went back to sleep. He tried to ignore the vomit smell of her breath and closed his eyes, willing his body into a somnolent state that was similar to human slumber.

Of Jell Fish And Giant Turtles

Jordyn awoke long before Aleta did. Dawn was on the horizon—a foggy lighter ball of color indicating where their sun should have been, and some soft gilding of the waves to the east. Not a bit of land or another ship was in sight, but they had stopped moving and the sail was reefed.

"What happened?" he called, sitting up and looking around. The surface of the normally rippling water had quieted overnight and they were surrounded by what appeared to be great gobs of translucent purplish pink bubbles that floated and bumped against the hull.

"Jell Fish drift," Hulda called back as she tried paddling some of them out of the way with one of the oars. "Water here is too warm these days, so they get terrible big and grow all at once. We can't get through them until they decide to move because they deaden the way, and there's naught enough of a wind to draw sail, so we're becalmed. It's a big colony, so tis going to take some time to make passage. Keep your hands aboard, their sting is full of poison and it kills flesh."

"W-what's going on?" Aleta asked as she awoke with a yawn and stretch. "Are we docking already?"

"I'm afraid not," Jordyn said with a distracted voice as he stared down over the side at the big pulsing blobs that were drifting all about them.

"We seem to have gotten into a rather difficult fix."

"I see that," she said, sitting up to look around at the bobbing things clustering about the boat. "What are they, some kind of water plant? No wait, they're swimming. What are those things?" She seemed very confused as she leaned out to look the roseate blobs.

"Don't touch!" he warned, yanking her back toward him. "They're some sort of invertebrate with a toxicant burn."

Aleta only understood the word 'burn'. "That's not a problem for me Jordyn," she said with a frown, and flicked a finger to light a bit of flame. Aiming it at the first jell fish, she extended the flame down until there was a sizzle and the thing shriveled and drifted dead. "See?" she told her fascinated companion, "I can burn them right back!"

"Not on my ship," Captain Hulda called back. "We want no fire witchin' aboard. We have cargo to think of."

The crew was looking at Aleta with fear in their eyes as she shrugged and sat back. "Suit yourself. I just wanted to help get us out of here."

"You're getting better at directing it," Jordyn said quietly, sitting down next to her and offering some dry biscuit and water, though she only accepted the latter.

"I learned the hard way," she said with a sigh. Looking out over the water, she spotted something almost as big as their boat, but rounder, floating in the water. There was another one a ways out. "Well, this is already pretty strange, but what are those things?"

Captain Hulda had spotted them too. "Archelon coming up fast! Now we're in for it!" They were benign giant sea turtles that fed on the jell fish, and they followed the blooms, but they were far from careful. Thinking them competitors, sometimes they rammed and capsized small boats. "All oars in the water. We're going through this," she said. The men took to their stations but couldn't make headway in the mess of bobbing globules that were fouling their oars, and the wind refused to cooperate.

"What we need is a decent wind. That would at least get us goin' hard against these things," the captain said with frustration. They were trying to move forward in a morass of heaving froth. The drag of the huge collection of bobbing spongy creatures was impossible to row through.

"I do think you should let my companion up front. She might be able to make us a path," Jordyn suggested as the men labored mightily, but the boat wasn't making much progress. There had been some ominous thumps on the bottom of the hull, which everyone hoped was just the drifting rounds of translucent bodies and not something more sinister like a surfacing turtle or the equally gigantic Mola Mola fish. Where there was prey, there would be predators, and the salt waters of Earth once again contained some very large and aggressive killers that had not been seen for ages. Creatures that would not normally be hunting humans could still manage to capsize a boat and drown them.

"All right, fine; but if she falls in she will die from their stings. For that I am not responsible, nor am I risking my crew fishing her body out," Hulda said in a matter-of-fact tone. Some of the Archelon were getting close enough that their enormous heads and fins could be seen very near the boat.

Aleta moved forward at a half crouch, and took a position up front. She leaned out as far as she dared, hanging onto whatever rigging she could grab, and lit a flame at the ends of her fingers. Directing it forward, she burned everything that was in their path on the port side, and then switched to starboard. By going back and forth, up and down the bow, she made enough room for the boat to begin to drift.

Some of the crew leaned away from her, or made a sort of three-fingered holy warding sign, but once the huge turtles were bobbing up all around, they quickly took up oars and began to dig in and move the boat forward. While only inches at first, the Curlew finally began to glide through the water once more.

A couple of times a giant flipper or head almost as large as Aleta would surface near the boat, and she had to wait until the huge creature moved on. To burn one of them, even by accident, would likely send it into paroxysms of pain that could upset the boat. Aleta would never have intentionally done that anyway, for the gentle, clumsy looking leather-backed giants of the water had large and soulful eyes, though Captain Hulda warned her that with their sharp beaks, they were aggressive if threatened.

"I've lost a few oars to those beasties," she said watching Aleta as the younger woman systematically swept flames back and forth across the surface. She always pulled back as soon as one of the big creatures got too near, drawn by the debris from dead jell fish bodies.

"I just find them interesting," Aleta said. Other than the man-made war mechs of the desert wars and Samanya the fire breathing behemoth who had given her the power to burn, she had never seen anything as large as the huge sea turtles.

"They shouldn't be here though," Jordyn complained. "They are from another era entirely."

"Tell them that," Aleta said with rolling eyes.

Eventually they made it through the majority of the jell fish. The gigantic turtles began to dive and swim away. The wind picked up again, and the sea became choppier. They were finally able to unfurl the sail. With that bellying, and some judicious rowing and rudder work, they left the jell fish bloom behind.

Aleta went back to her box perch and conceded to a bit of dry bread and fresh water, for after having expended some energy in producing flames, she was ravenously hungry; only hoping she'd be able to keep it down.

Tacking well, they began to make good time running before the wind in a faster sea. Aleta was still queasy at times, but kept what little she had eaten inside, and her spirits were far improved.

Late that afternoon, the shoreline of another small continent—actually a pileup of large islands slammed together by tsunamis and other cataclysms into a more compacted area—came into sight. It was a place that appeared to be slowly rebuilding itself, definitely doing much better financially and socially than the city they had left behind, although there was still no life in the former high rise buildings, and the new construction looked more like bunkers and barracks than housing.

A collection of ships large and small, sophisticated or ramshackle in appearance, were anchored out at sea or in bays deep enough to hold them safely offshore. The Curlew's crew moved the slender craft roughly parallel around the coast, heading for a covered docking complex that currently flew the sun face flag of the Solstice, the ship Jordyn and Aleta were going to be traveling on over the wider ocean. The Curlew crew ran up their own colors, the speckled bird with the long beak and legs on a blue field.

"We're almost in. They'll be sending another boat for you shortly," Captain Hulda called back to them. The sail was rolled and stowed, the mast unstepped, and they pulled up into the lower structure of the docking area via oars. After a few minutes of tossed lines and climbing, the crew made fast. There was a ladder that had to be grabbed and pulled down, and first Aleta, then Jordyn, climbed up to the waiting area of the sea dock while the Curlew's crew unloaded the cargo onto the barge pickup area.

Zephirine Merriwether

"This seems like it was designed for something else," said Aleta, looking up at tall, rotting metallic towers above squat, boxlike buildings that would house travelers during inclement weather.

"Yes. I believe it was some sort of mining platform for liquefied hydrocarbon material that used to fuel most of this world's technology before the wars," replied Jordyn. "A lot of the original base seems to be underwater now, but it does make a handy docking area, don't you think?"

"I suppose," Aleta said with indifference. She had no idea what a 'liquid hydrocarbon' was, and really didn't care to know. Looking down over the edge made her dizzy though. The lash of water against the sides of the platform, while not strongly felt, was hypnotic in a stomach sickening fashion. "Let's go inside a while," she suggested. *Anything to get this rocking, rolling motion out of my mind.*

Jordyn opened the door and they stepped up into the waiting room. There was a seating area that wasn't much more than rows of benches, and a tiny commissary selling teas and flatbread. Jordyn went to the window and mentioned what Captain Hulda said about seasickness aids. Once the counter help had looked at the embossing on his and Aleta's passage tags, they were given a small covered basket of supplies against their account. The ferry to the Solstice was running late, so they were to have a seat and relax.

"I'll be so glad to get out of here! All this waiting around is rather dull," Jordyn complained while Aleta was poring through her little basket, wondering what all the things in there were for. For someone who was basically immortal, Jordyn was not a very patient being.

"I'm perfectly happy right here," she said absentmindedly. The docking platform shuddered a little, but didn't have the rolling motion of the waves. It was a great relief to her to be sitting still for a bit.

Other people began to file in. There were several men and a woman, all obviously sailors, for they had similar sacks of clothing and belongings at their feet. They dressed very much alike, in some sort of colorless gray jumpsuit and dull blue hooded overcoats treated to shed water, their feet in short boots with slip resistant soles. The woman's hair was shaved as short as her companions, and she had the same hardened gaze and curt voice, though Aleta could not understand her. Jordyn could though, and by the amount of bawdy talk and joking around, he assumed they had all been on some sort of shore leave together.

There was only one other passenger, another woman a bit taller than both of them, and obviously well-to-do, for her clothing was neither old nor worn. She was clad in a long black coat with a row of metal fasteners over gray fitted breeches and black boots with low, blocky heels that laced nearly to the knee. Atop brown and curly hair that fell to her shoulders, she wore a brimmed black hat with some sort of goggles pushed up on it. Her collar was turned up and held in place at the neck with a flawless linen cravat of multiple layers. Ruffles of fabric stood out at the cuffs and neckline. Jordyn couldn't take his eyes off her, and stared at her ceaselessly.

"You're being rude, you know," Aleta complained, and nudged him with a sharp elbow in the ribs.

"I can't help it. I simply *adore* her darling outfit," he said entirely too loudly, so that everyone turned to look at the strange little man in tight dark clothing with a tattered lace fronted shirt, sitting next to the small, nervous, dark skinned woman. Jordyn ran his hands through the spiky blond hair atop his head and down over the longer strands, and sighed. "I wish I could find something grand like that for myself," he said sadly.

The woman in question turned to view him too, hazel eyes in a heart shaped face darkening from gray green to something nearer to brown. She pursed bow shaped lips and patted herself down. "Do you think it's too much?" she asked, her voice a low dulcet tone with a worried sound as she smoothed the ruffles down. Arched brows knitted together in a pucker. "I don't have to follow regulations like the regular Navy. I'm just a civilian sail settler."

"Oh, not at all! Why, I think it's an incredibly smart ensemble and makes you look smashing," Jordyn gushed. "I'm so terribly jealous too!" He bounced to his feet and extended a hand in greeting. "I'm Jordyn Orion, and this is my companion, Aleta Kalama. Please tell me you'll be on the Solstice with us," he added.

"Solstice is all 'at leaves the dock this turn, mate," said one of the sailors in a language they all could understand, but his companions elbowed him and made low, rude comments about talking to a 'blinkin 'eeshee'. Jordyn understood what was meant, but chose to ignore them.

"Zephirine Merriwether," the woman said with a polite nod, taking his gloved hand and shaking it. "Of the Bainsbridge Merriwethers," she added, as if that should mean something to them. "And yes, I'm berthed on the Solstice."

Aleta was standing now too, and she tentatively offered a hand and shook the other woman's cool and smooth one, feeling a bit tawdry and out of place with someone so finely outfitted and obviously much more well off. She pulled her own ratty red cape about her shoulders to hide the threadbare condition of her tunic and tights. Jordyn was completely smitten and almost seemed in shock, for he kept staring from his hand to the woman, with the most ridiculous looking smile on his face.

"You're a windmage, aren't you?" he said with excitement. "I can feel it in your soul."

"I'm a weather forecaster *only*," she corrected him with a quick shake of her head. "And *that* is strictly a science. Elemental magic is in the realm of the superstitious."

"If you say so," Jordyn said with a wink at Aleta, who blatantly disregarded his playful nature.

"What do you do aboard the ship as a 'sail settler'," she asked the other woman curiously.

"Oh it's quite simple really," Zephirine said with a slight smile as she accepted Jordyn's offer of a seat and tried to ignore his continual staring at her while she talked. "Ships like the Solstice depend upon a parafoil to pull them forward to help offset fueling costs. Thorium is an abundant enough element, but there aren't enough mines these days, and some of the best deposits are inside areas that are actively involved in warfare, or still too hot to enter. So it can be expensive to run these ships. What I do is read the prevailing wind currents. That allows them to adjust the direction of the parafoil for the most efficiency, and it saves fuel too."

"It sounds interesting," Aleta said with as much enthusiasm as she could muster, but couldn't picture herself standing around trying to decide what direction the wind was coming from.

"It can be," Zephirine said cheerfully. "Especially when a storm is brewing."

"That kind of accuracy must require a very specific set of technical skills," Jordyn said pointedly. "How long did you have to study for that?"

Zephirine grimaced and looked away. "It's... sort of a family business, I suppose. I apprenticed with my uncle, and now I'm... well, I'm on my own."

"So this is your first trial at sea then," Jordyn said quietly.

Zephirine leaned forward. "Alone, yes. But please don't tell the captain or crew about that, or they're likely to discharge me. You'll have to trust me when I say that I know my business. Yet while I have worked with mast sails on river boats, I have never sailed across the ocean before and that will be such good fun! I can't wait to see Columbiana. I hear they have devil winds out in the middle of the continent that can lift a body skyward." She seemed very excited by that, and two spots of color rose in her pale cheeks.

Jordyn squeezed one of her hands. "That does sound thrilling," he said with just as much enthusiasm.

"It sounds dangerous to me," Aleta said with a frown, finding herself increasingly irritated that this newcomer had all of Jordyn's attention.

Zephirine smiled broadly, showing lots of perfect teeth and high cheekbones, though her eyes looked wary and tired. "I intend to see all of Columbiana that is still traversable. I can usually get passage anywhere I need to go. You're welcome to come with me Jordyn and... What did you say your name was?" she asked the frowning little dark skinned woman sulking next to him.

"Aleta. Aleta Kalama," the other woman almost snapped, and her eyes took on a strange glow.

"That is a very pretty name," Zephirine said with a worried look, as she caught sight of the fire inside Aleta's eyes.

"Our ferry be 'ere," the sailor who spoke the common language announced and lurched to his feet, shouldering the strap of his bag. "Get along now or ye'll be left behind." He gave Jordyn a dark look, and then headed out and down the stairwell to the landing area, letting the door bang shut behind him.

"Well, we might as well get aboard too," Zephirine said with delight, bounding to her feet the same time as Jordyn and Aleta. "We're off to our new lives!"

"After you, ladies," Jordyn said, but fell in behind Zephirine as they climbed down to the landing just above water level, where the steam powered ferry with the paddlewheel was docked.

"*We're off to our new lives!*" Aleta said just under her breath in a mocking voice as she clattered down the stairs somewhat behind Jordyn, who was happily bantering on about weather forecasting and wind directions with Zephirine. "I *hate* her already!" she grumbled as she stood a bit apart from them, her little basket of seasickness aids in her hands. Aleta's sharp little chin was up, and warring emotions lit her eyes as Jordyn and Zephirine chatted like old friends while they climbed down onto the ferry ahead of her.

The ferry was no more than a glorified barge with a small cargo crane and pilot house on one end and the paddle wheel counterbalancing it on the other. The two man crew was a taciturn duo of regular naval grunts in jumpsuits and warm parkas. It was cold standing out there exposed. The wind whipping off the water flung spray in their eyes. Zephirine and Jordyn seemed to enjoy it as they hung on the rail, but Aleta shivered and her stomach heaved again. The passenger area had railings and a bit of a canopy to keep the weather out. She leaned against the back of a crate and closed her eyes.

She wasn't sure what the engine ran on, but it was noisy, though the ride was moderately fast. The water of the bay was a bit choppy with the wind, but it didn't take long to reach the Solstice, which was a long, wide cargo carrier. Most of its load was stowed in simple crates and barrels below decks, for there was no large dock equipment to load and unload it. Other than the small barge crane, all was packed away by deck hands. There were some stacks of weatherproof crates already chained down in racks on the deck, and a couple lifeboats, but large areas were mostly clear. The seas were often rough and with the threat of storms, monsters, and pirates, it was not wise to stack cargo out where it could be swept off or easily seen and coveted. There needed to be room for many to work, because transport and shipping had taken some steps backward in time. Most ships had decent sized crews again.

The Solstice

Once they were aboard, Jordyn, Aleta, and Zephirine found out that there were just two tiny empty cabins left available. The idea had been that the Sail Settler would have one, and Jordyn and Aleta would share the other. The captain however was a man of strong beliefs, and since Jordyn looked male to him, and he and Aleta could not show any legal documents proving they had filed a commitment agreement, he insisted the two women berth in one room, and Jordyn in the other.

"To keep temptation out of your mind lad," the red-bearded giant of a man named Rufus Jameson insisted.

Jordyn gave him a frustrated look as he walked off. "Just how much easier is this trip going to be on me if I am continually picturing their two young and nubile bodies half naked together in the next room?" he said with his hands on his hips and a disdainful sniff. That got him a hearty guffaw and a slap on the back from the grizzled mate, who went by Shepherd.

"Yer a regular bloomin' riot Orion!" the man said, "Oughta be an interestin' trip wit ye on board."

"Indeedy do!" Jordyn said happily, his spirits restored again. Excitement seemed to follow him everywhere. "I do so love adventures!"

"Well, ye'll have your have yer share of them afore this trip be over," Shepherd called to him.

~

"This would be awfully cramped for just one of us! I don't know how both of us are going to fit," Zephirine complained when her trunk was hauled in. The crewmen that heaved it up and carried it inside grunted and swore as they strapped it down, for the thing was heavy, filled with clothing, shoes, and other belongings. Zephirine thanked them warmly, and then shut the door behind them, and sat down on it with a sigh. "Well at least that part's done. But where are your things Aleta?"

Aleta looked at Zephirine uncomprehendingly at first, and then down at her only worldly goods, clutched in her arms as she sat on the bed. She had just a simple handmade rope sack tied with a drawstring, full of clothes and oddments, along with the little basket of seasickness treatments. "This is all I have," she said with a sigh, and then turned away. She stowed her things away in the little cupboard allotted to her with room to spare.

"Well, then, you'll just have to share mine," the other woman insisted, and opened the top of her trunk. "Let's find you something for dinner. I hear that Captain Jameson is going to toast our first voyage together."

Aleta stepped over and gasped, for within were some of the most elaborate outfits she had ever seen. How could the other woman afford so many changes of clothing?

"I… I couldn't wear any of that. They're just too… perfect!" she said with a combination of wondering desire and alarm. There was nothing in Zephirine's belongings that showed very much wear, except for some sturdy boots and a hiking outfit. Looking at each piece the other woman pulled out and held up was for Aleta like reliving the stories her mother's mother used to tell her when she was a tiny girl, of great buildings where every little shop inside had clothing or other pretty enticements that could be purchased.

"Where did you get such lovely things? I've never seen clothing so new," Aleta added.

"I get paid for what I do, and most times it's in trade goods," Zephirine said, hoisting out a linen blouse with long sleeves, and a full, gathered skirt of bright ochre. "Here, try these on, and if they fit, we'll modify them for you. I've never worn them anyway. They're a bit small for me, and I bet they'll fit you just fine." She helped Aleta dress, admiring her dainty proportions and slenderness. "You are such a tiny, perfect little thing. You're so lucky. I'm built like an old wooden piling."

Aleta spun around, and watched the skirt twirl around her feet. "I love it," she said happily, the glow in her eyes subdued, and her wariness gone. It was fun to feel like a young woman again.

"It looks good on you too. You should keep it," Zephirine said agreeably. She helped Aleta adjust the length of the skirt at the waist, and brought up the sleeves of the blouse by binding them at the upper arm and wrist with colorful hair ribbons. "We'll sew them later. I'll try and get needles and thread if there are any on board," she added. "Let's try this vest with it… Oh yes, that will do nicely," she added, digging out a moss green laced one.

Well attired, both women emerged from their cabin chattering like old friends, which warmed Jordyn's heart. It was the first time he had seen Aleta smile that much and she looked very fetching in her new clothing. He himself had freshened his own outfit and ran a borrowed comb of carved wood through his hair. With his second favorite coat and vest on, and the Eye of Providence safely stowed in his black ruffled shirtfront, he took one woman on each arm and they went off to dinner with the captain.

The Solstice was well underway by then, having left the port behind in the distance. Miles from shore, the sea was relatively calm and the sunset over the water gilded the surface where it streamed beneath the ever-present clouds. The engine hummed quietly, as they were under full power for now. It was planned that they be out of sight of land and other boats before they sent the parafoil billowing forward.

At dinner, Zephirine sat next to their red bearded, hulking giant of a host with Jordyn across from her. Aleta was on the other side of the large man, a quiet but observant shadow of her more ebullient feminine companion. Zephirine was animated and entertaining where Aleta was reticent and not often given to words.

Jordyn was completely fascinated with the idea of a ship being at least partially powered by a passive energy source. "Exactly how does that sail work?" he asked around a bite of savory roast meat, the last they'd be getting for a while, for fresh food didn't keep well aboard. They had the dining hall to themselves, the captain having declared it off limits for the duration of the meal.

"The idea is to let the trace lines loose when the winds come from the aft, and eventually it pulls the great kite forward," Jameson explained. "Adjusting the angle and paying out line allows it to ascend. That extra drag it creates helps to pull us along, and we can cut the engines somewhat

...they went off to dinner with the captain.

and preserve fuel. It also assists if we're pressed to make up time, and need the extra thrust."

"Why not deploy it right away?" Jordyn asked.

The captain was chewing, and shook his head before he swallowed and answered. "I can tell ye never sailed afore son. We have a sea breeze at night this close to shore," he added with a laugh. "It you wanted a braking motion or an air anchor that would be fine."

"So that means if the winds are going the wrong way, that sail would wind up behind us, and slow us down?" guessed Aleta.

The captain nodded and raised his clay goblet. "Yes missy, that's exactly what would happen, and at times it can be a blessing," he said with a wink before taking a long drink. In spite of his huge size and fierce demeanor, Aleta liked Rufus Jameson, for he was easy to understand and always a gentleman to the core. He didn't make her feel stupid.

"So how does it help pull us along better than a standard set of sails?" Jordyn queried, sitting back in his chair with one slender leg crossed over the other, swirling his liquor in the goblet.

"It flies on high sir," the captain said, but it was obvious he was not even sure why that helped. "And there's less sheet, which means less maintenance."

Zephirine jumped in. "Kites being what they are, they fly well above the surface winds you see," she said to Jordyn. "That upper wind flow is much stronger than the winds down at conventional sail level, and that creates more drag per measure. You'll see on the morrow when we get further out and can let it go up."

"I am going to enjoy this trip. There's just so much to learn!" Jordyn said, raising his glass, and they all shared a toast to a good voyage and calm seas.

The party broke up when the First Watch bell was struck, and the captain excused himself. Jordyn walked his female companions back to their cabin, and bid them a reluctant good evening, kissing them both on the cheek before retiring to his own room.

Back in their cramped quarters, both women undressed down to comfortable under things and crawled into bunks after saying goodnight. Zephirine dimmed the recessed lighting and they eventually drifted off.

Demons of the Depths!

It was late into the wee hours, near morning, when a strange bell rang continuously for a few minutes. Aleta, still all nerves, was instantly awake on the first peal, listening. Zephirine slumbered on across the room, initially oblivious as the warning bell was struck again. Aleta felt a hum and shift in the boat's course. They were now headed in a slightly different direction!

A light and patterned rapping came on the cabin door; *Jordyn*, Aleta knew from his past practice. She leapt lightly out of her bunk, wrapped her cape around her, and tiptoed over to open it.

"Something is happening out on the water, and I think we will be needed!" he said excitedly, holding an EL lantern of blue green high enough that she could see his face. "But you better both get dressed warmly, there's a stiff breeze and it's cold out here." He closed the door and hurried away in the night.

After shaking Zephirine awake, both women hurriedly threw on clothing, wondering aloud what the commotion was. Gathering their shared lantern with the blue green glowing central stone, they headed out on deck together.

"Douse those blasted lights!" the captain said in a low, commanding tone as they came abreast of him. "You'll draw them right to us, looking for shining baubles." Both Jordyn and Aleta shut the lanterns off and hung them in a safe spot, on pegs in the outer side of the aft castle.

It took a few moments for eyes to adjust to the darkness, but then they saw it. A jutting, rocky island, beautiful and serene, rose up out of the mist. As they drew closer they could see it held a city with tall shining towers of crystal and gemstone that shimmered with Aurora Borealis luminosity. Swirls of something phosphorescent made the water around it glow in stripes of many gaudy colors, reflecting an alien moon and stars that shouldn't be visible. It was incongruous where it was, in the middle of the open water late at night.

"That is an amazing sight! It's not everyday one gets to see a display that compelling. What do you make of this?" Jordyn asked the captain.

"Sea Fae Phantasm," the big man said with bland surety, his feet planted well apart and fingers hooked in his belt, where now his telephase ray pistol was tucked and a military issue saber hung. "They conjure something out of a dream, and then use it like a lure to bring ships in. The colors are a dead giveaway."

"So… that's not real?" Aleta asked uncertainly. The sweetest, saddest, most alluring songs with words she could not understand were coming from the island, and it was hard not to believe in its actual existence.

"No-no-no-no-no, it's far from genuine. What you're seeing is a macro-psychokinetic projected hallucination presented as a hologram," Jordyn postulated. "That takes a lot of skill!"

"If you say so," the small, dark skinned woman answered with a shrug. She had no idea what he meant.

"It's a manifestation of someone else's mind made to look as if it's really there," well educated Zephirine explained quietly, for she had understood what Jordyn said, even if he had gone to great lengths to make it complex. "You can tell it's not real because in that area there's no wind, no waves, and sometimes it flickers a bit. And remember, we shouldn't be able to see the sky like that. It's all make-believe."

"Trickery," Captain Jameson added in disgust. "Dark business this is!"

"It's still beautiful," Aleta said with rapture. To her, it looked like the shining city of ascended paradise, the way her people's shaman had described it to her before she became the Blessed Bride of their god.

"Do you suppose we will be able to meet them?" Jordyn asked the captain. He had some inkling of what or who was doing it, for it was the projection of an otherworldly place he had heard of but had never visited, and he was eager to learn what had brought Atlantean beings to Earth.

"You'd not be wantin' to get too close. The merfolk be a vicious lot, given to killin' when they don't get their way or they sees somethin' shiny they be wantin','" Shepherd said from the other side of them.

Captain Jameson agreed. "They are always unpredictable. We'll try and steer around them, but if they intercept us, we're prepared to trade or fight as the circumstances dictate," he added.

The men went off to their duties and battle stations, leaving Jordyn, Aleta, and Zephirine to contemplate the ghostly presence of the colorfully adorned island of Atlantis that was slipping by just to starboard. Jordyn, who had the heightened vision of the ascended, could see against the backdrop of optical illusion the splashing forms of a circling group of merfolk—all females, since they actually had the fishtails and never left the water for long. They were busily singing to life the exotic image as their male brethren swam underwater toward the Solstice, with the idea of boarding her and either demanding tribute or taking what they wanted.

"It seems to me that the female gender has the PSI abilities while the males are more the aggressors. And we are definitely in hostile foreign waters right now," Jordyn said to Aleta, as there were several quiet little thumps against the side of the ship, "So I think we'd be wise to prepare a defense." Looking over the side, he spotted grappling hooks fashioned from driftwood and scavenged iron were caught in various places, with lines of braided green seaweed leading down toward the water.

"Wait a minute—you're saying they're coming here to attack us?" she asked nervously as she started to glow a bit. Even her less acute hearing had picked up the sounds of several wet bodies slithering up the sides.

"Definitely. The way they're armed, they don't look like they care to trade or parley either," he quipped. He wanted to add that like some of the other things they had seen, the merfolk of far off Atlantis didn't belong in this world at all, but that was beginning to sound redundant after their recent adventures.

"Well, if I have to, I can fight them," Aleta said with a resigned sigh, as she took a stance and willed the flame to be ready. Swimming merfolk were now openly coming at them from all around the ship.

"Can you direct the flames outward so we can meet them head on?" Jordyn called aloud as a few heads with frilled neck gills and bulging eyes began to pop up over the rails nearby and scaly plated arms bearing wicked, jagged weapons pulled their bodies up. "I don't want to set the boat afire, but we've got to do something!" The bell was ringing for general quarters, and lanterns were being lit and hung, as the threat was realized and the need for complete darkness was over. Jordyn immediately had the Eye of Providence out and shining, held well above his head, illuminating the water all around them with the filtered brilliance of the stars.

Atlantean merman warriors were everywhere!

"I'll do my best, but there's a lot of them and only one of me. Not enough room for me to move around enough either," Aleta shouted in answer as she lit both hands afire. She began to pace back and forth, spiraling flames away from herself and out toward the rails. It did cause the first wave of the fish people's boarding party to move back, but the boat was long, and there were far too many of them for her to handle alone. They were determined to come aboard, and she would no more beat one back and move on and several more were swarming over the rail behind her. Some were already trying to loosen the cargo while others were engaged in battling with the crew.

~

Zephirine had immediately retreated, for she was not a fighter by nature and the scenario she suddenly found herself in bordered on madness. Knowing beyond a doubt now that there were such things as ocean monsters bent on killing humans was bad enough, but as soon as she saw Aleta's skin glow and her hands come alight, she wanted to run away and hide from this nightmare world of things that should not be. But everywhere she turned; there were continual threats of lurching wet bodies coming up and over the side of the ship.

In her terrified state of mind, she reached out unconsciously, and wrapped tendrils of a moist fog-bearing south wind around her like a shroud. But then Jordyn breathed into his hands and it lit something spherical and bright in his palm that threw beams of light around the deck. When he lifted it overhead, the piercing starlight made it harder for her to remain unseen in her veil of misty darkness. Anxious and confused, Zephirine scrambled away and watched warily from a distance as he directed the light outward, showing all aboard that an entire legion of the demons of the murky depths were closing in to attack them.

~

Jordyn felt the change in Zephirine as she enveloped herself in fog. He called out to her to come help, but she shrank fearfully away from him. He realized that the things he and Aleta were doing together in order to fight the mermen were almost as mind chilling to her as the nightmare creatures themselves, and he couldn't blame her for her confusion. He implored her as the keeper of the winds to come and join their defense, but there was nothing she wanted to do but run off and hide, crouching under cover until it was over. So he let her go to concentrate on the fight ahead.

Many more figures were swimming rapidly in their direction. Now that the mirage island was no longer needed, it was dissolving as it sunk beneath the waves, and the fish-tailed female merfolk went under with it. The males that Jordyn could see were more reminiscently humanoid than their mates—bipedal with a single set of upper limbs, and two bulging eyes in a broad, fish like face with no distinct nasal ridge. On a background of scaly plates of shimmering gray-green, their bodies glowed in various patterned hues. The brilliant, pulsing stripes and splashes indicated the mer-warriors' fighting colors. Dorsal fins, like sails with curving spines sticking out from them, went fully erect as arm and leg fins collapsed upon leaving the water. Partially webbed, six-fingered hands with long claws gripped weapons fashioned into fanciful shapes: daggers of wavy edged metal, curving wooden clubs studded with shark teeth, or spears and tridents tipped with the ivory of walrus and narwhal. With pulsing gills flaring and curved toothed mouths gasping, they were coming in from all around and swarming aboard, clambering about on thick, bowed legs with webbed feet as they hunted down the human crew.

There was shouting in the background and the ringing sound of cutlasses being drawn, the whump of pulse rifles or the sizzling hiss of interrupter beam shooting telephase pistols going off. The latter, more technologically advanced weapons, seemed to have only a small effect on stopping the merman advance, and so swordplay and clubbing became the preferred method of dealing with them. The engines were running hard, but the grim looking fish people swam fast enough to have no problem keeping up with the pace of the ship. They were starting to pop up everywhere and were hard to kill.

~

Captain Jameson was already engaged with several of them. His admittedly ineffective pistol had been lost to the swing of a trident, but his saber blade was flashing in the light of the Eye. He snarled like a big, red, hairy devil himself as he slashed, boxed, and kicked at the mermen trying to take him down. The deck beneath him was soon slick with the slimy ichor, severed body parts, and the tumbled guts of merpeople; as well as more human blood than any of them wanted to see.

The merfolk made either a booming hooting noise or strange bubbling sounds to one another, and suddenly they seemed to be swarming him, likely recognizing the red bearded giant of a human as the leader. He laughed like a madman and wrenched a trident from one, impaling and then ripping it free with a foot propped against the sagging body. He swung it up, taking the eyes out of another charging merman, while his saber never stopped hacking and slashing anything non-human that got too near. But more of them swarmed him and under the press, he was pained to hear one after another of his crew screaming in anger or fear for her or his life.

In minutes he and the first mate Shepherd, armed with a cutlass and telephase pistol, were back to back, fighting for their lives against a press of slimy bodies while trying not to fall on the slippery decks. The helmsman was down and they were beginning to drift off course. Some of the foul things had slipped below decks where sailors were forced to defend themselves and their vessel in narrow aisles and hatchways that lead to the engine room and the reactor beyond. As the untended controls lay idle and the engine slowed, more of the Atlantean warriors began to board the Solstice.

~

Jordyn was fighting where he could as with one hand as he held the Eye up so that others might see, for the merfolk had good vision in the dark but the humans did not. In the other hand he swung a quickly procured mop as he danced and skipped from one stack of crates to another. He knew Aleta was capable of defending herself, and as far as he could tell, neither the captain nor Zephirine had been caught yet.

Aleta was having some success with systematically incinerating mermen off the sides of the boat, but there were too many of them in inaccessible spots for her to continue that safely. If she set the boat afire, they'd all burn to death or drown. Her world was complete chaos as the bestial sea beings were now coming aboard several at a time, and they were all over the ship. She was kept busy racing after them and flinging fire around.

"Can't you talk to these things? Tell them to go away or something?" Aleta called frantically as she blasted flames at another trio of the slippery warriors, while a fourth one lumbered away from her. "I can't torch them all and we're losing too many people!"

Jordyn groaned. "I've tried every language I know, and believe me, I know hundreds of thousands." He ducked a vicious swipe of a twirling double bladed knife, batted the killing end free and came back to slap the creature in the face with the filthy mop before touching it with the Eye, and watched it shrivel into a husk of mummified death.

"They're completely ignoring me. Either they can't understand what I'm saying or they are utterly soulless." He suspected the latter, for the killing was brutal, systematic, and ruthless.

"Why are they here?" Aleta shouted as she set another afire. It staggered off aflame and hooting to leap over the side. "What in Hades' Blazes do they want?"

"I have no idea Dear One, no idea at all," Jordyn said with frustration as he parried a thrusting trident. "But if we don't get rid of them soon, we'll be overrun."

The Winds Of Change Do Blow

Instead of taking a stand with her friends, Zephirine's panic got the best of her. She was not a fighter by nature and had never seen a battle before. Covered in mist and fog, and quaking in fear, she backpedaled toward the shadowed part of the deck cargo area, praying none of the demonic things could see through her disguise. As the first incursion came over the sides, she scrambled farther away, desperate to find a more secure hiding place.

As she fled down the deck back toward the cabins, Zephirine passed a valiantly battling sailor. She wanted to stop and help the woman escape but had no idea how to do so, as there wasn't room to circumvent her furious knot of assailants. Within moments it didn't matter anyway, for the overwhelmed defender was being hacked to death by several of the ghoulish sea beings.

Zephirine shrieked in terror and the bulging eyes stared uncomprehendingly at her as she sped past, for they were only able to see the pillar of mist she had become part of. The wind of her passing by almost made the merfolk lose their footing as the unfortunate human sank to the deck, cleft in half diagonally and pumping out her lifeblood at their feet.

Trembling violently, Zephirine dove between two tall stacks of crates and crouched there, hiding. She was determined to stay under cover, and kept telling herself she could not do anything worthwhile in the fight. The safety of the ship was not her responsibility and she'd only get in the way. Zephirine tried very hard not to feel guilty when she heard brave little Aleta shrieking in defiance as she burned all the foul things she could reach, or breathless and agile Jordyn imploring her to come join with them in the defense of the Solstice before it was too late. Without a weapon other than her ability to read, capture, and manipulate the wind, Zephirine was not prepared to face those horrific murderous fiends of the deep.

The battle noise waxed and waned around her with a confusing cacophony of shouts and screeches, the unearthly calls of the fish beings, the buzzing zap and whomp of weapons fire, and the clash of metal edged weapons. Blood and other nastiness seeped in next to her, as she heard another body fall nearby. It didn't seem to be going well. The ship had stopped moving forward and was simply adrift. She curled into a fetal position, petrified that they were all going to die out at sea.

Zephirine had lived a relatively peaceful life, and had never seen such carnage before. She put her hands over her ears and sobbed silently. This was not a situation she had ever expected to be in when she set off to see the world. Her Merriwether ancestors had all been interesting, restless people that loved adventure: explorers or archaeologists, cartographers, surveyors, rainmakers, prophets, and philosophers. Many had the ability to sense and read the winds. A few could call them, but none had ever used it for anything more than making a living as some sort of sage. Some had been to war, a few had never returned. Most had died at a ripe old age after a couple of decades of retelling their tales. Their stories had captivated her as a child so much that she wanted to go out and make her own.

But not like this!

And now, on her first adventure, she was going to die at sea, and no one would ever know her legend. Something inside her rebelled at the thought that she would end her life without at least seeing some part of the rest of the world. It just didn't seem very Merriwether-like to be cowering under cover waiting to be killed. Certainly none of her predecessors had ever shirked a chance to be involved in making history. Thinking about her proud and adventuresome family helped bolster her resolve to get involved.

Well, even if I don't survive this trip, I'm not having a gutless end! She stood up slowly in that darkened hiding place, and the mist around her began to dissipate. *I don't suppose I can cause any worse damage and confusion than those things have.*

She could sense the winds above Solstice; she felt the air around her, and was aware of the way it shifted and swirled. Zephirine had never dared openly test the extent of her abilities in front of others, mainly because they were so hard to control and she'd had little practice using them offensively. If the superstitious ship captains she had dealt with ever caught her playing with the wind, they would have accused her of being an enchantress, an admission that would have gotten her executed in the place she had just left. It was something she herself could barely accept, and she had learned at a young age to hide her innate talents from the world. She was incredibly successful in her trade under the excuse that she was simply a very skilled weather forecaster. But now it was a matter of life and death for the people she had befriended, and so Zephirine Merriwether screwed up her courage to join them in the battle.

"I'm right here!" she called to Jordyn as he hopped from one stack of crates to another above her, trying to light up the ship for the desperate defenders and do his own share of the fighting. She darted out of cover and waved to get his attention.

"Hurrah!" he said, trying to beat his way through climbing attackers to get down to her. Leaping up and spinning to kick several in the face, he somersaulted about, zapping each one in turn with the Eye before landing feet first on the next stack of crates.

Zephirine already had problems of her own. As she stepped out into the open, one of the merfolk turned the corner and, spying her, swung up a great sword with an offset serrated blade. He charged awkwardly at her, intending to bring it slashing down on her head. She had no choice then but to defend herself with that she knew best.

Always aware of the air currents about her, Zephirine whirled to face him as she pulled the high, wild winds of the North into her body. Palms up, as if warding off his blow, she let it go all at once and thrust the raw power of a gale at her attacker. The sudden fury of the blast blew the merman backwards. He and several others were propelled off the boat and into the water with such violence that they were driven far below the surface with a great resounding splash. They would not be able to resurface for a while. That gave her a great sense of satisfaction, and another idea...

Clear of enemies for the moment, Zephirine Merriwether, with her long coat undone and hair flying wildly around her, rushed to the rail and took a deep breath. Concentrating hard, she quickly drew down swirling and powerful winds from far aloft and formed them into a vortex, refining it into a narrow cone that she directed down toward the water. As it picked up moisture, it became a waterspout that boiled the surface, sending the remaining merfolk that were trying to get aboard diving for cover. Running along the rail, slipping and sliding in the areas where merfolk had been injured or died, leaping over bodies and fallen weapons, Zephirine guided the waterspout along the surface, foaming the waves and cutting off access to the ship, churning the water around it so violently in such a tight gradient that nothing on the surface could survive. She took great satisfaction in grinding the merfolk back into the water every time a head popped free.

At Jordyn's call, Aleta slipped up behind Zephirine to guard her back and make sure the windmage was not attacked as she concentrated on forming a tightly whirling pillar of air that spun all around the Solstice, foaming the seawater so violently that the rest of the merfolk could not access the ship.

It was a late effort but it was enough to turn the tide of the battle, as the continual attacks grew thinner. A bloody and exhausted Captain Jameson and his crew finally began taking back their ship. The last merman body was tossed overboard just as dawn streaked the skies behind them, crimson and gold streamers of the sun showing below the clouds.

Four of their fifteen original deck crew had been killed and several more were injured, some seriously enough to be unable to continue their duties. Three more people would die that day alone. The haggard captain gave the order to once more bring the engines up to top speed, and they traveled quickly from that area where the ruined bodies of merman and hastily wrapped and shriven seamen floated together on the waves before they sank to a watery grave.

~

"Are you all right?" a tired and shaking Aleta asked Zephirine. The taller woman leaned over the rail. Bloodshot eyes in a pale face were closed, and her hands gripped the metal until the knuckles shown white. Behind them, weary crew members were sluicing and swabbing the deck.

"I'll live," Zephirine said raggedly, trying to make her head stop spinning. "I'm just exhausted. That took a lot out of me." She was trying hard not to open her eyes and see once again those dismembered dead that were bobbing and floating toward their wake. She struggled not to know that her boots were slickly coated with the reeking fishy slime of merpeople. "Oh no Aleta…" she groaned, "I think I'm going to be–"

"It's best to just let it go," Aleta said quietly.

Zephirine vomited over the rail for a few minutes, emptying her stomach until she was racked with dry heaves. Aleta stood calmly by a short distance away, arms hooked in the rails but facing away and inward. She was sympathetically quiet as she waited patiently for her sister-in-arms to deplete the final contents of her roiling stomach. After all, this was not the small, dark skinned woman's first battle. Her veteran status, as well as the freedom from the seasickness that had plagued her on the smaller boat, helped her feel a bit smug.

"It gets easier over time," she reassured Zephirine, once the taller woman had leaned back and wiped her mouth on her sleeve. "You were pretty amazing out there for someone who had never fought demons before."

"I'll take your word for it," the youngest of the Merriwether clan said as she staggered off for her cabin and bed.

Prodigious Possibilities

Crossing the great Sea of Alliance from the Unified Islands to the windy northeastern coast of Columbiana generally took a seven day period with a fully functioning ship, if all went well. The following two days were quiet and sobering ones for the crew of the Solstice. Another injured crew member died and a joint blessing ceremony for her and her fallen comrades who had been buried at sea made them all aware of just how vulnerable they were to the vagaries of their ravaged world in those difficult times.

Watches were doubled and assignments padded, for lost positions had to be covered. Accordingly, tempers flared and dark words were exchanged as overtired and emotionally drained people coped with their fears and grief while the injured struggled to regain health and strength with only the onboard apothecary and an all purpose infirmary manned by one very overworked doctor and several rotating volunteers. The two passengers and the Sail Settler, with their special abilities now known to all, were sometimes lauded as saviors and heroes, but also whispered about as mutant freaks.

To make up for the extra use of fuel, the parafoil was launched immediately the morning after the merman attack, and Zephirine took her place as Sail Settler, guiding the linesmen as how to adjust the rigging for the best drag. She did her best to surreptitiously align wind currents whenever possible, but the energy and concentration required made it impossible to keep the wind flowing strong and evenly throughout the day. She concentrated her efforts on the intervals when crosswinds threatened or storms brewed on the horizon, spending most of her time reading the fronts to take best advantage of them rather than fighting against them.

The cargo ship had no permanent shelter for its linesmen and Sail Settler, and so when clouds boiled in and it rained the second night into the third morning, the wind off the water was raw and cold. Zephirine was miserable and drenched even with a borrowed oilskin and the tarp they had rigged up between crates and the forward mast.

"Ye canna control the weather wi'd yer witchin' then?" Shepherd the mate asked as he shared a steaming cup of tea with a cold and drenched Zephirine, who had come in discouraged that they'd had to pull the parafoil down. The wild winds overhead were so fierce the rigging creaked and wanted to rip free, and once lost they'd likely never get the massive expanse of coated woven material back.

"No, I can't Davey. I sense the currents and read them and I can sometimes nudge a weaker feed into one a bit stronger. I can pull down some of the winds, and play with them here and there, but I can't change the overall pattern." She hugged the clay mug, letting its scalding warmth soak into her hands. Even with her overcoat and oilskin, she'd gotten wet and chilled to the bones.

"Half the crew says yer a sorceress, and we'd ougtha toss ye overboard. But I tells 'em ye fought them sea devils on our side, and te be glad o' that fact."

"Thank you," she said gratefully from beneath lowered lashes. Shepherd wanted more than thanks, but Zephirine never mixed business with pleasure. Besides, the man was not her type. She tended to enjoy the company of someone she could have an intellectual conversation with. Jordyn could be fun to talk to, but he was too quirky and effeminate for her tastes.

I guess I'm bound to wind up as a freakish old maid, she thought darkly as Shepherd left the galley.

That afternoon it cleared up, and while the skies still had the persistent ashy color of the ones over the land they had left behind, the scudding lower clouds had disappeared. The wind was still gusting, so Captain Jameson took his Sail Settler's advice, and didn't launch the parafoil again that day, for as she had predicted, the wind off the back of the passing storm was going the wrong way.

$\sim$

With the storm caused rolling and tossing of the boat, Aleta had been queasy most of the night and next day. She stayed in her bunk, refusing to do more than sip some tea and nibble at a large wafer of dry grain flatbread called hardtack. Zephirine was too busy to spend time with her, and Jordyn was always out snooping about, so she was often on her own. She really didn't care to socialize with the crew, for most of them watched her with looks that ranged from speculatively dark to pure fright. They were outwardly cordial, but avoided her whenever possible, and the small, thin, dark skinned woman felt the same about them. She heard the whispers whenever she walked past, and a couple of the bolder ones had asked her to light pipes. While she could have easily have done so, she declined, for it didn't seem dignified to her. Most of them saw her as haughty and unapproachable, and a favorite watch game amongst the men and the female crew members who preferred the intimate company of other women was inventing new and more intricate ways to 'shag' the dusky little spitfire without being scorched.

Jordyn seemed completely unfazed by the negative commentary and speculation his presence invoked. As always, he was more focused on the purpose of the trip. As weather permitted, and sometimes even when it didn't, he watched Zephirine at work, and realized she had no idea of the full extent of her abilities. He felt she could do a lot more manipulation of the air currents than she was presently, with simply focusing on wind direction. It was something he hoped to work with her on, if she would agree to join him and Aleta in his search for the other two elemental beings he knew had to be somewhere on Earth in this turbulent age. He was pretty sure she would come along with them, for Zephirine seemed lonely and at somewhat of a loss for where to go next once they docked in a few days.

One thing that bothered him was why the Atlanteans were on Earth again. They had made several appearances in times past, as mankind's historical accounts would attest. This group had seemed madly determined to kill everyone off and go through the cargo.

"They've been getting more aggressive as time goes on," the red bearded captain told him as he changed the dressing on a wound to his ankle that had left him hobbling a bit. The galley was the general purpose room for just about anything, including their infirmary in times of trouble.

"So you've had issues with them before?" Jordyn asked pointedly.

"Not like this," Jameson answered, with a sour expression that knitted his sandy red brows together and made his weather-beaten face appear a bit cross-eyed. "In the past we would bring aboard trinkets and beads, and then toss them over the side as they approached, and that would be enough. But after a while it would draw an excess of them in and they started demanding more 'n more, so now we just give only when we absolutely have to. But this was something I've never seen the likes of. It was as if they wanted to be aboard and look for something... or someone," he added, glancing over at Zephirine and Aleta talking softly in one corner by themselves.

"And you have no idea who or what that could be? Something amongst the cargo perhaps?" Jordyn suggested, following the captain's gaze.

Rufus Jameson paused to stroke his red curled chin and his eyes got a

...he watched Zephirine at work...

distant look. "I thought of that, and I've been poring over the manifest, but there's nothing in the freight all that out of the ordinary. You or the ladies didn't bring anything unusual aboard did you?"

"Not that I know of," Jordyn said thoughtfully. Aleta had very little of her own, but Zephirine had an entire trunk of clothing and oddments he had not looked over. It was something to think about.

~

A warning bell rang again the fourth day out, this time during the light hours. When Jordyn and the girls came on deck, they were shocked at what they saw.

Nothing.

"It was over there," an excited junior officer, with the stump of his right arm in a sling, told the frowning mate as he pointed off to the port side with a trembling left forefinger. "A long neck and a hump, just sticking up out of the water. It looked at me and then dove down again." The man was shaking with excitement as well as from the stimulants he was taking for the pain.

"Sea monsters?" Jordyn asked Captain Jameson when he wearily clomped over with spyglass in hand.

"It would appear so," the big man said sourly. He was beginning to think this voyage was cursed, for he could already see the water boiling off to starboard with a school of fish being chased by something large. He called to the helm, "Slow the engine, let the kite do the work for now." He turned to Jordyn and said, "I've no desire to hit one of these things at full throttle. They tend to get frenzied about protecting their own, and that can be dangerous. There's enough wind to keep us moving steadily."

"I see one!" Jordyn said excitedly, pulling Jameson's arm around and pointing. Actually there were two of them, great long necked, mottled skinned beasts that came to the surface, huffed out, swiveled their heads around, and then dove down again. "What are they doing?"

"Periscoping," the captain said, handing his glass over. Jordyn could have used the Eye, but accepted the rare granting of a privilege. "They want to know what we are."

Jordyn sighted through the glass and with his superior ocular ability, was able to watch one of the creatures surface. It had a slick dusky blue and olive green patterned skin with a pale underside. A huge rhomboid flipper tossed up spray as it lazily rolled sideways and dove again. "They're really quite docile, and seem to be hunting either fish or squid," he said, handing the glass back over. "Are they any danger to us?"

"Generally no," Jameson said, but he looked troubled. "But there always be others that hunt such as them, and that is what we will have to be on the lookout for."

"That would be a terrifically big creature, unless they hunt in packs," Jordyn said with a speculative tone in his voice.

"On all accounts yes," Jameson answered in a flat tone, and walked away.

Aleta, sufficiently recovered from her seasickness, joined Jordyn on the deck, and they wandered over toward Zephirine. Shepherd was hovering nearby, as he usually was these days, since the boatswain had been killed and he was the next best rigger, but he wandered off when they passed by.

"What's out there now?" the small woman asked dryly.

"Sea monsters," Jordyn said cheerily, pointing to one in the distance.

"Yipes!" Aleta said unhappily. "That thing is pretty large."

"Not as big as this one," Zephirine called from closer to the bow. They hustled over to where she was leaning against the rail. There, a heavily variegated head half the length of her own body was visible just under the surface. Barnacle dotted jaws clamped down on a large squid, which inked the water. The tip of the muzzle broke the surface and raised its nostrils above to breathe in and out. The long necked creature lifted its head to chomp and gulp down the squid and then looked around, eyeing them carefully before diving again. It was fascinating to watch, and just a bit frightening, for the parts of it they could see were enormous.

"These are some sort of plesiosaur. They aren't supposed to be alive anymore!" Zephirine said to Jordyn in a worried tone.

"Yes I know. They were once part of Earth's early prehistory," he confirmed.

"Then why are they here now?" Zephirine asked with a perplexed look.

Glancing around, he saw that Shepherd had gone off to his other duties and the rigging men, though nearby, were not within earshot if they spoke quietly. Jordyn moved in and beckoned Aleta closer.

"It's a bit hard to explain Zephirine dear, and we mustn't alarm anyone, but time and space in the vicinity of Earth have become quite scrambled. Things aren't occurring in exactly the order they should."

"What?" both women said rather loudly and he shushed them.

Aleta protested, "That makes no sense!"

He sighed, and acted as if he was talking to children. "First of all, you can't think of time as something that just passes and then it's gone.

It's always out there," continued Jordyn, "Just moving away from us. Interstellar space is where everything floats around, so to speak, including the energy of things past this life."

"That's superstitious nonsense!" Zephirine insisted. "Things die all the time, and then they're gone, but this never happens!" She pointed to the plesiosaur, which was in the process of grabbing another squid. "They have been extinct for ages. Now they're back, and you're trying to tell us that's because they fell out of the sky?"

Jordyn waved her to silence. "Yes, actually, I am. Things do die, but normally, only the energy of those with high level sentience have a chance at being reborn in this life, for they are the ones with immortal souls. Their energy vibrations are also the most... um, lively," he added with a shrug. "To put it simply, the sudden extinction of so many of those with energetic souls during the last couple of generations of warfare and ecological upheavals on Earth put a lot of strain on the fabric of the Universe. It sort of bubbled outward and actually ripped open in places while contracting in others. Of course that tends to destabilize the areas around it, and those voids must be filled."

"Which means?" Aleta asked with dread, not sure she wanted to know the answer.

Jordyn shrugged. "Well, just that some parts of Earth's past history, along with chunks of other places and times, have been pushed inward through the space/time continuum, and have dropped back inside to fill those empty spaces. So things have sort of become muddled, and now you have an inhomogeneous mixture of life as you've never known it."

"That just sounds... *bizarre*," Aleta said, shaking her head in disbelief.

"The truth of things generally is," he reassured her.

"So we could experience more of this type of anomaly," Zephirine stated uncertainly, and she looked ill at ease.

"Yes," he answered quietly. It was a worry for him too, and he wondered what else they would have to deal with.

"And you're saying that our past is always out in space somewhere?" Zephirine pressed him with a quizzical look, trying to grasp the concepts he was presenting. Aleta looked at them both blankly, but then stared back in the water at the plesiosaurs.

"In a way yes; but only the deceased part of it that has become all energy without mass or matter. If you could view it, it would appear like a..." he had to hunt for the right words, "a mirage of what was. Except when things get reanimated like this, all you'd normally see are ghostly three dimensional images. Once objects or beings come back through our time though, if there is room for them, they tend to reform into solid material."

"What about the future?" Aleta asked quietly. "Is that out amongst the stars too?"

"No," Jordyn said with surety. "We're still solid matter, so we haven't made a future yet. Otherwise time would have gotten away from us and we'd all be long since dead."

As confusing as it all sounded, that was a sobering thought.

The creature they had been watching dove suddenly and swam off, with many others following it.

"I never expected to see anything like this," Aleta said as she began to walk back toward the Sail Settler's enclosure, with Zephirine right behind her. "Not stuff from Earth's distant past."

Jordyn brought up the rear, deep in thought about what was going on in Earth's seas.

Zephirine was about to perch on the stool Shepherd had provided her with, and indicated a couple of small empty crates and a big coil of rope next to her that her companions could sit on. "Well, I've sailed a lot, back on the rivers and lochs of the UI, and I can vouch that life on the water is always fascinating. The ocean is like a huge laboratory–"

She never got another word out, for directly ahead of where they had been standing, a huge black striped, green form suddenly surged up twenty feet into the air. It caused a resounding wash onto the deck and the ship rocked slightly as the behemoth broke free of surface. It was two thirds the length of the boat and almost as heavy, with tremendously long punishing jaws filled with curved teeth the size of thick daggers. It had clamped tight on the now limp neck of a plesiosaur and blood pumped in streams down across its long snout as the big predator tipped sideways and went under again, unfortunately snagging the line of the parafoil and taking that with it.

Even More Problems!

"The sail!" Zephirine yelled as she leapt to her feet.

Crewmen rushed forward and tried to drag the lines free, but before they could gain control of it, the creature's weight snapped them, and the high flying kite sailed off on its own.

"This trip be damned! I have never seen such a foul run of luck!" Rufus Jameson complained darkly when he was informed. With no extra kite aboard, they would have to depend solely upon the thorium supplies for locomotion, something that was certainly feasible, but costly in both monetary and time considerations, since they packed only as much fuel as they needed for a sustained moderate pace. "We'll be an extra day out or more now, and the speed will suffer," he said darkly.

"And I'm basically useless, so I bet I won't get any further compensation," Zephirine said unhappily once the captain had stomped away, grumbling to himself. "The contract states I only get paid for 'services rendered' beyond the cost of my housing."

"You can still read the winds for them, tell them when a storm is coming on," Jordyn said hopefully. He was actually not sorry, for he and Zephirine would have more time to explore her talents now that she would no longer be watching the sail.

"I suppose," she said with a sigh. "I just don't know if they'll pay me for that."

~

There was a lot of muttering later that day, and black looks at the trio as they entered the galley. Increasingly often, they found themselves isolated with no more than their own company.

"What is it with these people?" Zephirine complained over a dinner of dried meat and vegetable soup with fresh baked bread. "They act like we're the cause of all their problems."

"They're not used to humans with outworld powers," Jordyn said around a bite of bread. He did very much enjoy human food, no matter how humble it was.

"I don't understand why we're so different," Aleta said mournfully, picking away at her soup. She was not crazy about the salty dried meat, which tended to make her nauseous.

Jordyn stopped chewing for a moment to think about the answer before he replied. "You have become who you are because your talents are needed here," he said simply. It was hard to explain the reasoning of the godhead, which tended to vary depending who was in charge at the moment.

"I was just born this way," Zephirine said with a shrug. "A lot of people of my line had some sort of affinity for forecasting, and some could feel the winds. I don't think anyone could call them though."

"You're not calling them as much as channeling them through you," Jordyn corrected her. Zephirine made a face and looked like she wanted to say more, but Aleta interrupted again.

"Were you sent to find us?" she asked Jordyn, for she knew by then that he was a star traveler and some sort of celestial being.

He shook his head, for his mouth was full again, and then swallowed. "No. I came here to look around for myself, and in the process stumbled across you. It's a long story, and not one I can go into here, but let's just say I know there are supposed to be four elemental beings in any age of upheaval, and they offset the four Apocalypsians, who are always up to no good. So far I've found two of you and one of the four dreaded ones."

"That was Samael." Aleta fairly spat the name, recalling with distaste the Dark Father of the undead she had fought against with Jordyn.

Zephirine looked at them both mystified, having no idea what was meant.

Jordyn nodded, chewing and swallowing before he said, "The Apocalypsians are the destructors, and you Elementals are the rebuilders."

That got Zephirine excited, and her voice raised. "Oh, so this is about balance, like in alchemy! If I'm Air, and she's Fire," she said entirely too loudly, pointing at first herself and then Aleta, "Where's Water and Earth?"

"Out there, somewhere," he answered quietly, trying to ignore the stares and grumbling of the crew members.

"One thing I don't understand though," Zephirine said as she pushed her bowl away and sipped bitter tea sweetened with crystallized honey. "I only pull the winds down, I don't generate them. How does Aleta create the fire without burning herself all to cinders?"

Aleta looked uncomfortable at the question and her flickering eyes gave an impression of the turbulent emotions within as she fidgeted under their scrutiny.

"She likely doesn't know how it works," Jordyn said in a low voice. "But you have to understand that the fire she calls is not of this world; at least, not initially. The same dimensional rifts that allows the energy of things past into this world, also allow memories to pass in and out again." He looked over at Aleta as he spoke, and saw that warning light in her eyes as her skin began to glow a bit. "It's the past fire she has known that she calls back again, Zephirine dear, and now that she can control it–"

"I can direct and use it, rather than letting it consume me," Aleta said dryly, getting to her feet and stalking away.

They watched her leave, and then Zephirine leaned toward Jordyn. "She… she burned like that in the past?" She looked aghast at him when he nodded affirmatively.

"And I thought my life had been difficult," she said, draining her tea and leaving the galley after handing in their dishes.

Jordyn smiled knowingly as he went back to his own cabin to contemplate what it might have been that had drawn the mermen of the north seas to them.

~

Zephirine went looking for Aleta and found her on the forward part of the ship, staring disconsolately into the dusk.

"I'm sorry if I pried where I shouldn't," Zephirine started to say, but the small-boned, dark skinned woman shook her head, trying to hide the tears, which got her a hug. "It's not so bad. We'll get through this," her taller companion added.

"You don't understand," Aleta said, trying to pull away. "You at least appear normal. Your touch doesn't hurt people. The fire is something… something I'll never forget. Or the fact that I'll never have a real life with a man, children, or a place of my own in this world. I can barely contain it sometimes. I'll always be a freak. I'll always be alone."

Her voice dropped off as she sobbed and started to grow alarmingly warm.

"You have us," Zephirine said quietly, holding her closely despite her heat. "We'll be like a family. And I *do* understand, because I know how hard you have to work to control it, hold it in, and not let anyone get close. I can't be myself around others anymore either Aleta. I'm always going to be like the sideshow act in the marketplace, unable to travel without pretending to be what I'm not. We'll just have to help one another through it."

Although unconvinced, Aleta realized Zephirine was facing similar problems. "Thank you for being my friend," she said quietly and they both relaxed.

Once composed, these two women of different backgrounds, but with the same sort of mystery surrounding their lives, stood together with arms locked around each other, and watched the last rays of the sun setting in the west.

They were there until dark, when a very concerned Captain Jameson sent a crew member out to look for them, and suggest that they get safely within their cabin for the night.

~

A great expanse of tattered fabric billowed and slid down the front of the metallic cylinder. It snagged the gondola platform that was slung below the zeppelin body, and hung there, flapping. The deck crew of Goliath cut the tangled rigging free, yanked it aboard, and folded it up. Two of the air raiders strapped on gear and took it down to the deck of the flagship themselves, using the partially furled cloth as a parachute, while the engineer steered the craft to hover over the metallic vessel in the water below, dropping line and harness to bring them back aboard again after they reported to their leader.

"Bloody blasted at last, we have a bit of fortune tossed our way!" Katherine Bellows, captain of the Grendel, swore happily at her good luck when several of her crew laid out the fabric and remaining harness on the deck before her. Pickings had been lean lately and this was a find. She didn't recognize the parafoil's charge symbol, but the design showed it was from a Unified Islands merchant class vessel, and the fact that the other ship would now have to depend on its engines alone for locomotion made it fair game. The UI thorium powered cargo ships were slow maneuvering even at full throttle and her smaller, low-slung steamer could easily outrun them.

"Figure the wind direction, and set a course to intercept," the muscular woman with the clockwork left arm said. She tied a scarf over her blonde bob to keep it out of her eyes, and then checked her cutlass and blaster. "We're going to get us some trade goods after all."

Men ran to do her bidding, many far bigger and stronger than she was, but the erratic young woman with the commanding presence paid that no mind. She could out drink, out cuss, and out shoot most of them and had no problem making an example of anyone bold or mad enough to challenge her, by gutting them on the deck and watching them die in agony. But Crazy Katy, as she was known, was fiercely protective of the crew members loyal to her. Even for pirates, they were paid well and rewarded promptly. Most were devoted to her, and just about any man aboard would give his life on her behalf.

Handing off the folded sheeting, she stalked confidently along the iron decking, tall boots with tight fitting trouser legs tucked down inside making a definitive clicking sound no one could mistake for anyone else.

The air raiders were lifted back up aboard the zeppelin hovering overhead, and it drifted sideways until the little engines on each side revved. Once under full power, Goliath looped around to the aft as the ironclad's sails were furled and the loud humming engines of the Grendel were fired up. When the twin stacks began to belch oily smoke, they started moving low and sure through the water, like a big black iron predator.

Alongside, orders were shouted and mirror signals flashed, as the frigate and caravels with them hoisted sails and tacked into the wind a short ways behind, flanking the Grendel. Sea and air power combined as the fleet of the pirate queen of the Columbian Coast set out to meet a ship they expected to see on the horizon anytime soon.

～

Later that afternoon, the Solstice was still a day or two out from the coast when the watchman called, "Ship Ho!"

Shepherd the mate, always alert, came to the port side with a spyglass and peered through it, frowning heavily. "Full throttle and take evasive action t'starboard. Have someone ring general quarters. I'll go inform the capt'n we've got some company coming in fast." He handed the glass to the next-in-command with a nod and hustled down aft again, taking the metal and wooden stairwell two clattering steps at a time into the hold where the galley was. The general quarter's bell was ringing just as he ducked in from the passageway.

"Begging yer pardon Sir," Shepherd said with a salute to his superior and a nod to Jordyn and the ladies who sat nearby, "but there be a steamer ship approaching fast a-port. She's lyin' low to the waterline, wit' a frigate and a couple of caravels flanking 'er and something airborne bringing the rear. She was just running up a red flag wit' a black demon face when I had the glass. Definitely be pirates."

"We're having the most damnable luck on this trip!" Jameson said with a groan as he pushed his food away and heaved himself to his feet. "I think you'd best stay down below ladies while I go check this out." As he hitched up his belt and grabbed his weapons, sailors were already swarming up to weather deck level, manning the helm or the long range guns. The captain of Solstice stomped angrily from the room, Jordyn right behind him.

"I'm not staying down here!" Aleta said, getting to her feet.

"Me either, they're going to need us," Zephirine agreed, and followed her small, lithe sister of fortune up the stairwell and onto the deck.

The Solstice Fights!

Like a giant metallic shark skimming through the waves, the Grendel came chugging right at Solstice, her gun turret rotating forward as she headed on an amidships collision course. A loud chuffing of her steam-fired engine indicated full speed building as the stacks puffed a thick and sooty vapor. Those aft could hear an audible bubbling of the screw as she let off some ballast and rose to ramming height.

The forward thrust battering head of the ironclad ship's reinforced bow extension was aimed right at the Solstice's waterline below the rubbing strake. Crazy Katy knew that should be where the cargo vessel's engine room was located. Hit that way, it would flood slowly. Taking on water in that area would shut down the engines and eventually overload the reactors, but give her people plenty of time to deal with the crew and offload whatever cargo they wanted. They would then either scuttle the big ship or blow her sky high afterward. She had no concern about what happened to any survivors. They meant nothing to her. Crazy Katy was a cold hearted, ruthless corsair with little left to lose. Pirating was more about reputation and boasting than whatever plunder they obtained and dead sailors told no tales.

"I take it you have no intention of surrendering?" Jordyn asked Rufus Jameson as he followed the big man around, watching him bark orders and issue pep talks. "There are several of them out there, so you must have a plan." At least he hoped so!

Jameson glared at him. "Master Orion, I own this ship, and our cargo is my sole responsibility. I'll not give in to piracy," he said darkly, his mind already set on the next step. "They know we can't hope to outrun them, but they've no idea how we're armed or they would've fired on us first. We'll leave that detail unrevealed until the last possible moment. We take out their flagship first, and worry about the others if we survive that."

"Spoken like a true fighting man," Jordyn said with a nod of approval as he felt in his shirt for the Eye.

"I've got some military time in," Jameson admitted, flipping back a sleeve to show a service tattoo, "which is where I picked up our armaments. We'll let them think we're going to make a run for it, then bring her about and let them have all we've got to give."

"They'll have to get almost on top of us for that!" Jordyn said in a worried, yet admiring tone. He had snooped enough to know what the Solstice had for weaponry, which were lightweight guns meant for arming coastal patrol ships. "They might ram us first!"

"They'll try, but I know my ship. The Solstice will take it. We'll still be moving, so that makes it more of a glancing blow, and close quarters is when we can most likely cripple them. They'll think we're unarmed and be hoping to board us while we're starting to take on water, not expecting us to make a stand."

It was a reasonable plan. Chancy, but well enough thought out. "My team and I will do whatever we can to help," Jordyn offered.

"I thank you, but you'll serve us best by staying out of harm's way. Just don't be doing anything rash that might give away the fact that we're armed. And that is an order," Jameson snapped without a backward glance as he strode off.

"We will use discretion, sir," Jordyn saluted him as he walked away, for the big, red bearded captain had some real battle acumen, as well as nerves of steel. Even if they managed to debilitate the ironclad ship and stop her from battering a hole in their side or blowing the Solstice out of the water, they would still be boarded and outnumbered. There would also be the other sailing ships to contend with. In the distance, a giant airship of some sort was looming. Below its metallic skinned cylinder, a platform deck was slung, lined with armed pirate crew members. It was going to be a formidable, lopsided battle, and in spite of Jameson's assurances, Jordyn knew that the three of them would be sorely needed.

He held a hurried conference with Aleta and Zephirine on how best to use their mutual talents as shock troops, once they were free to join the fight.

~

When the Solstice accelerated, the speedier Grendel piled on even more steam and gave chase. The quick little pirate caravels ranged out like flanking hounds while the frigate came sweeping in at an angle to cut Solstice off, her gun ports opening. Large bore cannons protruded, pointed directly at them as an ominous threat.

The fact that the pirates were cocksure in depending on the heavy plating of their leading vessel to protect them was the one thing Jameson knew he had in his favor, for his still hidden guns were not equipped with conventional shells.

At the captain's orders, the helmsman made a slow and barely perceptible, wide-arcing turn with the less maneuverable cargo boat; its engines at full throb. Once in position, the Grendel was almost on them at port side, and the frigate 'Lizzie Borden' was coming up quickly on the starboard. Hastily set up gunners with heavy pulse rifles on swivel tripods bolted to drill holes in the plated deck took positions on several points along the length of the Solstice. Some were a deterrent to keep pirates from boarding, the others took aim at the zeppelin as it came in, attempting to knock out some of the airmen ahead of time.

Striding confidently amongst his crew like a tall and noble warrior king of old, red haired and bushy bearded Rufus Jameson was more of a calming and rallying influence than his contemporary aboard the Grendel. His booming voice could be heard even above the surging engines, the nervous shouts of concern, and status reports. He knew he was leading sailors who were not necessarily fighting men and women, but the Solstice crew was like family and they would stand together as one. So he appeared steadfast and seemingly undaunted by the nearing danger as he clomped around ordering things here, bolstering spirits there, and reassuring everyone that their captain had confidence in them and was not at all ready to raise the white flag. It was well known in those waters that to give into any pirates, especially Crazy Katy Bellows, was most likely to earn a watery early grave. None of the rogues of the sea wanted their ships described, or the often inflated accounts of their deeds diminished, so the usual ending to a successful raid was the killing off of the plundered ship's crew.

The Grendel was almost upon them at that point, and overhead, the Goliath was coming in fast too.

"We're all gonna get tossed around here mates, so just hang onto those guns. Once the shooting starts, we want the advantage of first fire," he warned the deck gunners, bracing himself with his back against empty racking, and grabbing hold with a meaty hand.

A young man nearest the captain, likely several years well under twenty and on his first ocean voyage, quaked with dread anticipation as he watched the low slung, dark colored ironclad vessel approach, his eyes wide with fear.

"You're looking at too big a picture boy," Jameson called to him in a low voice. "Sight someone aboard through your optics and make that enemy the only thing on your mind. Then, when you've had your shot, choose another."

"Yes sir," the young gunner said, saluting and settling in to pick a target as the black ship steamed up.

When the Grendel hit Solstice in the side, one of the nearest gunners went over backwards and cracked his head on the deck. The next nearest was staggered, but their captain stayed on his feet. The boy in front of him was swayed, but he stood his ground proudly, and his pulse rifle shot straight and true. The range was too long for a kill with that sort of weapon, but he knocked down the first three men he hit.

~

At Shepherd's orders, gunners below decks waited until they could hear the Grendel's engines. Only then did Solstice's port side hatches open. Particle cannons were rapidly slid up on their tracks and locked into place, barrels protruding from the open ports. They weren't nearly as massive as the turreted gun the Grendel carried, nor had they the range, but they were much more pinpoint accurate and less likely to overshoot.

And they were totally unexpected.

Jameson and Shepherd had prepared the crew ahead of time to take a hit, and just before impact, the mate warned the gunners to hang on to the breeching lines and gun handles to stay upright and on target. Everything was going to depend on those first critical shots. The two port side guns were trained on Grendel's turret and the wheelhouse. As the frigate Lizzie Borden heeled into a turn to present her own gun ports, someone called the range to starboard. The battery on that side also appeared and readied, each gun fixed on a crippling target of the pirate ship.

There came a deafening metallic boom and the screech and scrape of metal hitting metal, followed by the groaning sound of plating under stress. The impact of the hull being rammed by the Grendel shook Solstice, tossing crew and objects around like leaves in a gale. It popped rivets and bowed the heavy reinforced plating over the nearby engine room, and some of it shifted and shipped water, but it mostly held and the bilge pumps kicked in immediately.

"FIRE batteries One and Two!" shouted Shepherd before he even managed to pick himself up off the floor and wiped the blood of a forehead wound out of his eyes, for he'd had little to hang onto. "*Steady* on Three and Four—make them shots count ladies and gents. We'll not be gettin' a second chance!"

The animal roar of Captain Jameson ordering defenses on the upper deck preceded the staccato whumping of pulse rifles going off overhead. The frantic sounds of gunners and other crew members shouting to one another drifted down through the open hatches. The particle cannons whined sickeningly as full charges built up and they began to fire crackling, buzzing beams of bluish bursts that turned purple as they met and heated their targets.

In the first few critical minutes the Solstice did take out Grendel's helmsmen and steering in the collapsing pilothouse, along with a gunner and mate when the ironclad's cannon barrel melted. The charge they were frantically loading had just touched off and it blew up inside, bulging the thinner-plated can of the gun turret outward and warping the shaft of the turret gear below. That crippled the pirate ship's ability to fire on them or effectively steer, but it was not powerful enough to stop its forward motion. Grendel kept bouncing into the Solstice, battering over and over in the same area, which was going to eventually open a seam wide enough to cause serious trouble.

"Keep firing on her! Just pick a spot, mates. I'll be headin' to the engine room so's we can get this old girl out of here before they beat a hole in her side," Shepherd shouted, and headed toward an aft end hatch as the second set of whining charges began to build.

~

When the Solstice's starboard gun ports flipped open, the alert crew of the frigate was able to maneuver her fast enough to avoid a direct hit from one ray, though the other vaporized her port side's protruding cannon barrels and scored deeply into the wooden hull, igniting the powder magazine. But the acting captain aboard was savvy and experienced. Even as he steered her away, the gunnery crew of the Lizzie Borden made sure the fire was out before it went too far and blew them up. On the fly, damage to her timber structure was assessed and patches with tarred canvas and lath were being put in place. He was about to bring his starboard side around with cannons ready to fire when he received mirror flashed orders to back off and take a stance out of gun range. As soon as the particle cannons were neutralized, he was to bring her back in and have a boarding party ready.

~

"FIRE batteries One and Two!"

"Our chance to get in the fight is coming fast," Jordyn warned Aleta and Zephirine as they braced themselves against the wall of the crew cabins, out of sight for the moment. "We have to give Captain Jameson his opportune moment to surprise and cripple the lead ships, but there are far too many pirates out there and too few crew members aboard to run the ship and defend it at the same time."

"So, we're going to be boarded again," Zephirine stated nervously.

"At least these are humans," Aleta reassured her, spread fingertips already spouting wisps of flame as her eyes started to glow. After having fought the undead and mermen, that significance was important. Human antagonists were far easier to kill.

"We'll need to get right into this," Jordyn warned them, pointing upward as the zeppelin soared overhead. He pulled forth the Eye of Providence, noticing with satisfaction that as she strode forward confidently, Aleta's eyes now had a fiercely incandescent backlight and her skin was glowing too. "I'll man the high parts of the ship, the bow and stern. I can reach them faster than either of you."

"I'll take the starboard side," Aleta told them, thinking she'd have a better chance of taking out the frigate with fire.

"I guess that leaves me the length of the port side," Zephirine said uneasily. She seemed much less sure of herself than Aleta was, but after drawing a ragged breath, she stepped out as well, taking a defensive stance with hands up as she tried to control her breathing and still her pounding heart. She watched with grave concentration, drawing the air currents down until a sudden breeze whipped her hair and coattails out around her.

She was ready to fight.

"Good hunting ladies!" Lithe and graceful as an acrobat, Jordyn Orion leapt and vaulted from rail to rail, deftly ascending atop the aft peak cabin area. Once up high, he raised the Eye of Providence, and willed into it some more of his essence, to charge it with the light of the stars he'd passed through. It shot radiance all around the Solstice, bathing the ship in the silvery white light of the heavens.

We stand together and ready, come what may!

Boarded And Overrun

Aboard the Grendel, the fact that they could no longer control steering and had lost their only big gun had not gone unnoticed in the chaos moments after impact. Knowing that the Solstice's particle cannons would need a few minutes to recharge, Crazy Katy raced down the deck like a fury, dodging pulse rifle bursts that splatted all around her as she shouted orders in a hoarse voice. She had a brace of blasters in cross-draw holsters on her slender, muscular torso; along with a dagger on her belt and cutlass in the baldric-hung sheath at her side. The hydraulics of her left arm whizzed and clicked as she pointed here and there, ordering men about.

"Cut the engines!" she shouted. "Signal Goliath to get us some cover fire! Send some of the air crew in and have them disable and capture those blasted particle cannons! I want those guns!"

Men and women scrambled to do as they were ordered while dodging shots on the open deck. Katy Bellows yanked one of her officers aside.

"They're still moving, so get the damn hooks out there, snug us in, and be ready to board. We'll bring the frigate up soon as we have their big guns down, but tell them to hold their fire. I don't want that hulk sunk, because once I've had my pick of the cargo, we're taking her for ourselves. And get those airmen aboard her now!"

The crew raced to their stations, some of them signaling the other boats or the airship with mirror flashes, in between dodging vicious counter-fire. A few fell to the deck twitching, as pulse blasts from Solstice's riflemen shut down their nervous systems. A couple would never move again.

Several well aimed gas and smoke bombs were shot through the open gun ports from modified grenade launchers. They shut down the Solstice's lower cannons quickly as gagging and gasping gunners stumbled around choking and cursing, their eyes streaming and swelling shut.

The Grendel's harpoon guns, confiscated from whalers and modified to shoot long shafted grapnels, went off with a boom and a puff of smoke of their own. Overshot to drop over the Solstice's side rails, hooks and rope dropped in, were yanked taut and made fast, lashing the Grendel up tight alongside.

Once signaled, the Lizzie Borden drew in on the starboard side, and when close enough, hooks went out from her as well. The airship Goliath hovered nearby but not directly overhead, so as to stay out of rifle range. Pirates armed to the teeth began to glide down on folding wings of canvas, leather, and whalebone; weapons in hand and murder in their eyes. Jettisoning their flying gear once feet touched deck, their first objectives were taking out the deck gunners, and then they would head below decks to confiscate the cannons.

With the particle cannons shut down, the Solstice would have to depend upon hand-to-hand combat defenses again. The problem with that was there were at least five pirates already boarding for every crew member left. From several directions, enemies swarmed up and over the sides or dropped out of the sky. Most were armed with at least a blaster as well as a club or blade of some sort. The airmen flying in dropped impact flash and concussion grenades on the gunners, and while they did small damage to the ship, they tended to knock defenders down.

And so the boarding began. All around the Solstice, pirates came over the rail or down from the sky with murder in their eyes and the love of battle and plunder in their hearts.

~

Rufus Jameson snarled as he drew his telephase pistol and unsheathed his saber. Solstice's big captain charged right in to meet the pirates. He was soon fighting like a madman, both weapons continually in play as he fiercely defended his ship. He had tried to prepare the crew for whatever attacks they might experience, but in those post-war days, it was impossible to know what kind of weaponry and gadgets might have made it into the hands of the myriad of potential brigands and aggressors roaming the land and sea. The zeppelin was something he had not expected, but it would be dealt with in time. For now, he had a mostly civilian crew to defend, and they needed their captain amongst them.

There was a metallic clink nearby and a rolling sound, followed by several more on the deck. An experienced soldier, instinct made Jameson dive for cover shouting, "Fire in the hole!" Unfortunately the majority of men and women aboard Solstice had little such experience. Most nearby had no idea what was going to happen, and simply turned to stare dumbly at him before scrambling away.

As the first concussion grenade blew, the two closest gunners were knocked down. The farthest one got back to his feet, but was reeling around, digging at flash-blinded eyes. The other man had been very close to where it went off, and he lay as if dead with scorched skin and blood running from his ears and nose.

Jameson had dodged into the container racks to avoid the grenades, covering his eyes and ears as they went off. Still partially deafened, he lurched out again quickly, and headed for the helm. He was not about to let control of the ship fall into pirate hands, and there was something stowed away in that area that could help take out the airship.

The young gunner whom he had reassured earlier screamed in pain as he went down beneath several assailants, fighting for his life. The captain rushed back to beat off his attackers and then secure the weapon. The red bearded giant of a man fought like a demon to get near the gun; hacking, slashing, blasting, punching; and eventually wrested the plasma rifle from the hands of a grinning sky pirate, shooting the man in the face with the telephase pistol. At point blank range, it vaporized his head. A partially melted helmet fell off the limp body with nothing above the shoulders but the blackened, cauterized stump of a neck. The headless body seemed to get the message that it was dead rather slowly, as it only gradually relaxed and let go of the gun handles, toppling onto the deck. Ignoring what was left of the dead pirate, Jameson quickly stepped up to man that gun, swiveling it to take down two more of the airmen diving in before a club over the head sent him reeling to his knees and he knew no more.

~

"I jist took their capt'n down, Dickie!" a triumphant woman's voice said with glee just before she was thrown forcefully backward against the rails, upending and going overboard. Zephirine Merriwether advanced on her, hands up and hazel eyes flashing as she gritted her teeth and blew one after another of the attacking pirates coming through the air or climbing onto the deck off Solstice and out to sea.

The loss of life and ongoing carnage was wearing on her. "Go away!" she screeched hysterically as she rushed at them. "Leave us alone and just go away!"

Another pirate, a small, swarthy man with a scarred cheek, rushed over to finish off the captain with Jameson's own saber, which he first wrenched away and then hastily stabbed into the gut of the groaning, injured boy that lurched forward in defense of his commander.

"I'm sorry sir. I did my best," the boy said as he sank to the deck holding his pierced abdomen, blood all over his shirt and hands, and his eyes wide with pain and shock.

"You're a good lad," said a deep voice, thick from a haze of pain due to a fractured skull and internal hemorrhaging that was giving the captain double vision. "Never... give... up!"

The scar faced pirate wheeled and with the captain's razor edged saber, took off Jameson's arm just below elbow as the half conscious man shakily raised his telephase pistol. The shot went wild and Jameson slumped back in a shower of blood and agony. The pirate hovering over him was ready to issue a coup de grâce and had begun to sink the sword tip into the struggling man, but jumped when a voice behind him said, "Tag-you're it!"

The surprised man whirled to see a grinning blonde haired, androgynous clown with a glowing ball in his gloved right hand. Jordyn Orion had materialized behind him, and he touched the confused pirate with the Eye of Providence, dispassionately watching him writhing and stiffening as the energy of life was drained away. He became a wailing ghost without a corpse, which Zephirine blew away in disgust.

"Goodbye Dickie. This world will be a better place without you in it," Jordyn said, before kneeling at Jameson's side with Zephirine, whose hands were full of blood as she ripped the captain's shirt free and tried to tie off the his severed arm to staunch the gushing from the stump.

"I don't think the sword punctured a lung, but that arm is gone, and he's bleeding out fast!" she said in alarm, indicating the ragged tear in his shirt and the alarming pool beneath the man.

"Well, we can't have that," Jordyn said simply, squatting next to her and drawing the Eye up close to peer through it. The brave and able captain's life force was almost spent, but his soul refused to give in.

"Jordyn, can't you do something for him?" she asked, looking up and raising a hand abruptly to blow a couple more advancing pirates away.

"There's not a whole lot left of him at this point, but I'll see what can be done," he said with some doubt in his voice, for he did not have his staff, which would have made emergency healing much easier. "Watch my back dear, I'm got to at least close this up or he'll die right here." No surgeon, he ran the Eye of Providence over both wounds, sealing not only the exterior but the vessels inside that had been ruptured. It was far from perfect, but at least it would prolong his life long enough to get him out of there.

"What are we going to do with him?" Zephirine said in a worried voice. The pirates were still coming on strong and she was kept busy blowing them out of the way.

Jordyn looked up from where he squatted next to a very pale faced and unconscious Jameson. "I can take him out of this and get him safely elsewhere, but he's weak and I'm positive he won't survive the trip. Can you handle things down here on your own?"

"I'm fine. Go! Do whatever you need to," she said grimly. Getting to her feet, she strode forward to chase down another pirate group.

"That's my girl," said Jordyn with a smile that turned to a groan as he grabbed the bloody, severed arm, and heaved Jameson to his feet. "My stars, you're heavy!" Arm around the mostly comatose man, he dissembled and pulled both their essences into the Eye of Providence, knowing full well that by doing so, he was dooming the red bearded captain to his death. But Jordyn also knew it was absolutely necessary, and that Rufus Jameson would not have it any other way. There was something hidden atop the quarterdeck that only he knew how to assemble, and that item might just be their salvation.

As his captain disappeared with the Starman into the glowing bubble, a nearby sailor saluted weakly as he dragged himself over to his gun station and tried valiantly to stand, ignoring the choking blood in his throat that made him cough, and dribbled both from the corners of his mouth and down the front of his breeches.

~

"We've got these buggers now!" Crazy Katy Bellows chortled as she reached out with the clockwork arm and grabbed the rail with its three claw-like metallic fingers and opposable thumb. The padded cup and torso strapping that held it tight to her stump and shoulder strained as the mechanism whirred and clicked. The arm straightened and its superior strength swung her up and boosted her over the side, to land on her feet like a cat. Her personal guards were right behind and beside her, but she motioned them off, for there was hardly any crew left to fight.

She stalked past an empty cargo rack and brought her blaster up immediately. With one shot to the chest she took down a blood streaked and grimacing crewman who rushed at her swinging a jammed pulse rifle, butt end first. The first man had not even hit the decking before a wild uppercut of the metallic fist broke the jaw and nose of another one charging in and laid him out several feet back. She laughed contemptuously as he sat up dazed; spitting blood and teeth all around before a vicious kick to a temple with a steel toed boot put him down for good.

Striding confidently aft now that it was apparent that the Solstice was mostly overrun, she spotted a dying crew member who still was cognizant enough to answer questions, though wounded badly enough not to have much fight left in him. She reached down with the mechanical arm, grabbed and yanked to his feet a young man slumped before his now empty gun tripod, holding a gut stab wound. His frightened eyes were glazed with pain and his fingers dripped red with his own blood. There was plenty more of it around him, most of it not his. Unmoved by his plight, the pirate captain hiked him off the ground, and slammed him up against a crate, where she held him fast. A glare from dark brown eyes without pity or remorse bored into him, as she demanded in a low growl, "Where's your blasted captain?"

"I dunno," he said weakly, his blue eyes rolling in shock and fear. "He got hurt some, but I think I saw him flying off aft with that Star Man while the two Wyrding Ladies were killing off your sea rats. But he left this for ya—"

Knowing he had but one chance, he pulled out a hastily retrieved, blood soaked telephase pistol from his shirt and shot her in the head. Unfortunately the weapon had lost its charge already, and what was left in it was not enough to do more than sting. It hit her point blank, but her helmet protected her, though the optic sighting lens of her goggles shattered. "That's from Captain Jameson!" he said weakly and spat blood in her face, knowing he was as good as dead anyway.

"Pah, you're a half-witted, weakling dunce," she said contemptuously. Other than heading aft, most of what he said had made no sense to her. Satisfied she'd gotten all she needed to know from him, Katy let the metal fingers clamp down on his thin neck until they throttled him. When his face turned blue and he stopped struggling, she tossed his limp body aside like trash, and after pushing her useless goggles up on her forehead, stomped off the remaining half length of the ship, a blaster held ready.

~

Everywhere were the sights, sounds, smells, and carnage of battle. Dead and dying pirates and defenders lay all around, some of them decapitated or otherwise dismembered. The stink of burnt charges, fresh spilled blood, and scorched flesh assaulted the nostrils. The clash of steel blades, the pounding of feet, and men and women shouting or shrilly screaming oaths and pleas, filled the misty air. In knots and singly, grunting and heaving bodies still wrestled and fought to best one another. Where the fighting was over, crates and barrels were being dragged forth and pried open, as the pirates began to plunder the Solstice.

The ship had lost half her remaining crew in those first few desperate minutes of furious hand-to-hand fighting. The particle cannons had been taken with little resistance, as there had been heavy casualties on that poorly manned lower deck. After shedding their wings, the sky raiders came in equipped with canister masks and infrared goggles able to see the stumbling defenders in the fog of gas and smoke left by the bombs tossed inside. The gunners all lay dead.

Only Shepherd the mate escaped the gun hold with just a blaster burn or three. He made it through the hatch just before the engine room beyond before locking and bracing it and throwing closed the thick blast doors. It pained him to leave his gunners to their fate, but Captain Jameson's orders had been explicit: protect the engines and reactor at all costs. That small but all important part of the crew was the least prepared to defend themselves, for they dared not leave their posts.

When all forward motions ceased and Solstice began to drift, he swore aloud, because that meant the pilot house was taken, and while he drew breath, the captain would never have allowed that to happen. Jameson was likely dead then and that meant Shepherd himself was now acting captain.

He issued low orders to the three remaining crew members in the engine room and reactor area before opening a floor hatch. Leaning in to look around, he let himself down cautiously, dropping down into the lowest cargo and bilge area. Mostly muffled, echoing sounds of the fighting overhead made their way in, though there were already pirates trying to pry open the heavy loading hatches above him. Shepherd moved noiselessly and with great vigilance amongst the stowed cargo, blaster at the ready, but so far there was no one around. He made his way gradually back toward the hidden access hatch that lead upwards toward the stern of the boat, intending to find out Captain Jameson's fate and get back into the fight.

A Ghost Of A Last Chance

Atop the weather deck, a rather vaporous and fading figure who was once the captain of the Solstice worked alone, resolved to make his final stand. Only his stubborn determination not to give in to the pirates and his love for the ship and her crew had kept him within the world of the living. His objectives were twofold: to sink Grendel and the frigate, then use whatever means he could to take out the airship. Focusing was hard, for voices called to him, breaking his concentration.

Rufus Jameson had to keep reminding himself of what he was here to do as he went about his setup. His own muttering was a continual low drone. "Shepherd is a good man, but asks too many nosy questions. He always wanted to know what all the drill holes in the decks were for. I suppose he knows now!"

Jordyn Orion kept watching for danger, though he knew that only an immortal would be able to see them in their current state. The captain kept looking around too, expecting to be attacked again; not realizing none would see him now except the slender, similarly ghostly figure that stood behind him with the bit of glowing starlight in his right hand.

"It's bloody cold up here," Jameson complained peevishly. "I can barely feel my feet, and for some reason my right arm tingles."

"I know Sir," Jordyn said in a soothing tone. The big man was beginning to flicker now, and Jordyn breathed more life into the link between them. "Please, just show me how this is done," he encouraged, knowing the poor confused soul had no idea of his less-than-viable status. Time was of the essence, for the sea god was summoning, and what was left of Rufus Jameson would soon heed His call and pass on out of the mortal world. Already some of his movements were not much more than a blur and Jordyn could see through him. The severed arm was back in place, but was not functioning well. That seemed to bother Jameson, for he stopped to stare at it now and then. "Our time grows short Captain; please explain to me how the device works."

Jameson sighed without having any real breath to exhale, a sound like the rattling of old parchment. "In the days before the war, when we docked ashore and cargo was mostly small lots, these little deck cranes were the only way to load fast. During the wars, we run out of fancy weapons, and modified them to fling charges at enemy vessels. Very crude, and a sneaking dirty way to fight at that! You can't see it until the arm goes up and the charge is on the way, but line it up straight and you should be able to hit anything nearby."

The captain rattled on about his memories to no one there, for at that point Jordyn had understood what needed to be done and left him to it. He was already headed down to confront the pirate leader as she came looking for her contemporary to force his surrender, not knowing yet that it was already too late for that.

If she reached Jameson and let on that she wasn't able to see him, the captain would immediately realize something was wrong. After his passage into Jordyn's energy bubble, his Earthly body had all but dissipated. What little life force wounded and dying Jameson still possessed had passed from the world of the living to the limbo of the unshriven dead. He existed only as a spirit now, his ghostly presence still capable of piecing together and setting up an impromptu trebuchet that only he understood. At least he would be able to do that as long as he believed himself still alive. Jordyn hated to trick the Captain's ghost, but if not for that, his knowledge would die with him.

"And look here! See how it swivels and locks in place, so you can quickly go after more than one target?" Jameson's ghost rattled on with pride as he set up and armed it, not realizing he was now completely alone.

~

"This tub is as good as mine," Katherine Bellows declared, as she tossed the twitching corpse of the substitute helmsman and the hacked-up woman who had died defending him out of the pilot's cubicle. Standing in blood, she snorted in satisfaction. The helm was no more than a retrofitted antique setup with a small hand wheel and a bank of dials and compasses, gyros and buttons. Simple to use and easy enough to override once they had taken control of the engine room and reactor below.

She shut down the controls and motioned a couple of her guardsmen in to hold the area, then went looking for the captain—for if he still lived, he knew for sure by now his only choice was to surrender in defeat. If he did so quietly and called what was left of his people off, they would all get a noble and quick death. If not, she would have fun chopping them up and feeding them bit by bit to the sharks and other predatory creatures that were surely by then circling the crippled ship, drawn by the scent of blood and the splash of dead and broken bodies hitting the water.

The Solstice was the biggest ship she knew of having been commandeered by pirates successfully, and that fact gave her the greatest sense of triumph. It had been a stroke of luck for her that the cargo vessel had been in a previous battle where they lost their kite sail and evidently part of their crew, for some of those left aboard had shown obvious injuries from fighting. That bit she would never make public, for the tale was far more impressive with the odds stacked evenly.

No longer would the filthy bilge rats at port stops poke fun at the wild eyed blonde spitfire with the clockwork arm of brass and steel, and the belligerent attitude of an untamed wild animal. Crazy Katy had taken the biggest prize of all: a hauling ship that could be refitted to smuggle just about anything she could get her hands on, including war mechs, armaments, and highly precious uranium and thorium. That kind of service was the real currency in these hard times.

She exited the small bridge, noting something afire down the port side and trying to get a better look at it. It was the sails of the frigate, which Aleta had finally managed to set afire, and Katy swore heavily. "What the blue blazes started that?"

"Oh, just my associate, who has been busily burning your crew to charcoal," a voice above her said.

Though momentarily blinded without her goggles, Crazy Katy immediately spun and got off a couple of shots. She crouched defensively as she drew the second blaster, for there was a sudden light of a dazzling brilliance—something she had never seen the like of before.

"You must be the one-armed pirate captain they've all been going on so much about," said a mocking voice that was hard to define as male or female, but seemed to come from all around her. "I've been just dying to meet you."

"Well, you're half right, because you're going to die for the meeting!" the woman snapped back with a grim curl of lip as she fired both blasters in staggered bursts. It was tough to follow the gaily hopping and vaulting figure vaguely outlined in that blinding luminosity. The target appeared to move up and down the stairs and all over the rails of the aft castle. She never scored a direct hit, though the light did dim briefly once or twice. The burning sails of the frigate were soon forgotten. "You might as well stop running around like a coward 'cause I'll be taking you out eventually," she warned in a frustrated tone.

"Not this day!" Jordyn Orion said merrily as he somersaulted down and landed lightly to face off against the pirate queen, who tucked aside one blaster in favor of the cutlass, and squared off against the one she figured the dying lad with the nulled sidearm had called the 'Starman'. The foolish looking idiot with the teased blonde hair and foppish clothing appeared completely unarmed except for the glowing ball in his left palm. His impish face held a smirk of insolence, though under arched brows, aquamarine eyes heavily encircled with kohl glimmered cold and hard.

"Tsk, tsk, such a disappointment," he mocked her with right hand on a slim hip, guessing correctly that her ego was as large as her ambition.

"You're not nearly powerful enough to take me on—just a pugnacious little girl with a huge ego pretending to be a nasty old pirate. You might want to take some time now and pray for guidance from whatever being it is you worship," he suggested coolly. "This folly of yours is doomed to failure." He wanted to keep her attention on him, in hopes of giving Jameson enough time to set up.

"Pah, now aren't you the big talker!" She gave a mocking laugh, never taking an eye off him as she circled for a better angle without leaving her back exposed, for the brilliance of the starlight orb made her head pound. She half suspected his stalling was letting someone else get in place for a kill shot at her, so her senses were all alert. "We'll find out how much you can back that up, won't we?" she retorted with a sneer. How she hated men like him; so overly confident, and self important enough to think they could order everyone else around.

The blaster came up again quickly in her left, the mechanical hand with a pincer finger connected remotely to a corresponding neural sensor implanted in her brain, slowly squeezing down on the trigger at the same time her cutlass came up defensively. It was hard to see with the brilliance of the orb in his hand, so her plan was to take the arm holding the starlit globe off at the wrist and then finish him with the blaster. She fired a dusting-back shot at him.

But Jordyn laughed and easily sidestepped it, as well as the quick follow-up swipe of her cutlass.

The cutlass flashed in her hand. She had never lost a fight to a man before, though some had cost her dearly. Even in her anger, she had noted that the blaster bolts she fired at him seemed to be drawn toward the glowing orb in his hand, where they quickly dissipated. She emptied the entire charge into it anyway, figuring it might overload his weapon and cripple him somehow. Jordyn just stood his ground sneering recklessly, as all her previous conquests had, before she killed them.

"You can't kill me with energy—I eat it for breakfast," he said with a waggling forefinger.

"Fine," she said, "I'll gladly run you through instead!" Since he appeared to be made of flesh and blood, Katy Bellows tossed the dead blaster aside, and with a roared oath, lunged at him with the wicked curve of her sword raised in her right hand and the claws of steel that terminated her artificial limb raking for that mocking smile.

Jordyn chuckled grimly, though his eyes never lost their glittering viridian intensity. Distracting and drawing away the pirate captain was what he had planned on doing as soon as he spotted her in the aft section. Now that the cannons were taken and the Solstice's lower decks under siege, he would do anything he could to give the ladies a solid opportunity to turn the tide of the fight, and whatever was left of the crew a chance to regroup. He dodged and feinted with Crazy Katy, trying to draw her off. Whatever was left of Captain Jameson was setting up a bit of a surprise for the airship Goliath, which still spewed pirates and small arms fire down at them. If he could just get close enough, he might put this pirate harridan out of the battle altogether.

And the captain is almost always the heart of the crew, he reminded himself as he leapt over her latest sword thrust and tried to touch the Eye to her, but she whirled fast and nearly took his hand off with the blade. She was obviously after the glowing orb, for it was all about bragging rights and prizes won with this one. That gave him an idea. He suddenly dropped the Eye and made as if she had somehow injured his arm, pulling it back before backpedaling away as if now frightened of her cuts and thrusts.

Instead of scooping it up immediately as he had hoped, she moved in with cutlass swinging, warding him off before drawing the larger military issue blaster. Thumb clicking the lever to vaporize, she took a steady bead on his heart.

"You must think I'm still green and stupid," she said, yanking the trigger several times in rapid succession, noting with satisfaction that the blasts went straight and true at Jordyn and did not deflect to the shining orb now lying loose on the deck. She laughed mirthlessly as he bucked in agony before crumpling into shining bits of matter that rapidly winked out.

"Well, that was easy enough!" Crazy Katy laughed in derision, holstering the blaster. She reached down for the Eye of Providence with the mechanical hand. "Now let's find this bloody tub's captain and end this thing once and for all." The brass clockwork of the arm whirred and the hydraulics hissed lightly as steel fingers closed around the now dimming orb.

The Final Stand

With armed pirates still occasionally dropping out of the skies, as well as clambering over the sides via the ropes, what was left of the Solstice's

...she took a steady bead on his heart.

defenders were far outnumbered—in many cases previously injured—and desperately in need of a miracle. Whatever Katy Bellows had intended, she was winning by sheer numbers alone.

When Jordyn had leapt up atop the aft cabins, Aleta and Zephirine had spread out to use their own particular talents to assist wherever they could.

Eyes glowing brightly, Aleta screamed the ancient war cry of her mother's people as she willed the flames hot and bright around her. She raced lightly into the fray, whipping tongues of flames into the pirates swarming over the starboard side and flinging them at their ship. She managed to dodge swung blades and most of the weapons fire as she ruthlessly burned the bloodthirsty shouting men and women who were climbing the ropes and pulling themselves up over the sides. She plowed through them time after time, trying hard not to think about how killing other beings with fire was becoming a way of life for her.

Several fires were started aboard the frigate before they backed off out of range and used the landing boats to board Solstice. Leaning over the rail to burn those was dangerous, so Aleta had to concentrate on just dealing with the boarding parties.

The frigate had a large group of pirates aboard and beating them back kept her busy. Aleta raced up and down the starboard side of the ship fighting them off, trying to burn their boarding ropes without setting part of the Solstice on fire in the process. She was hit once by a pulse bolt from above and it staggered her. She had to let go of the fire for a moment, almost losing her life in the next as a hastily swung cutlass nearly came down on her head.

Fortunately, a Solstice crewman, though seriously injured with a sword wound to the side and a blaster bolt having taken out his right eye and burned the side of his face, had enough fight left in him to heft a heavy, long-handled gaff used for dragging freshly caught fish aboard for the galley. With two quick swipes he took down the screeching woman with the cutlass, hooking her arm back painfully with the first one, and then ripping it free to tear her face open with the other swing. She hit the metal deck screaming and writhing in agony. Aleta burned her where she lay, then nodded quickly to her staggering but triumphant benefactor, before moving on to the next knot of assailants.

～

When Jordyn had left with Jameson in his arms, Zephirine was once again plunged into a melee of heaving, struggling combatants. Her mood was grim and she fought to remain emotionally numb to the horrors, though this time she was better prepared for the bloodshed and mayhem that ensued. She was still very sickened by it all, but the adrenaline rush of self-preservation and the need to protect her brethren aboard drove all other thoughts from her mind.

With a low pitched reverberating shout of defiance, she sprang into the midst of the port side fighting again, hands up and winds blowing out from her. She dodged wrestling bodies locked in combat and dying people reaching out to plead for help, and concentrated on keeping the pirates from advancing. Walking resolutely through blood and gore, she forcefully blew attackers over the side and back down to splash into the water below or to land hard on the iron decks of the Grendel, hoping one of them was the pirate captain.

Zephirine wanted to create another waterspout like the one she had used to drive away the Atlantean mermen, but was having too hard a time concentrating. There was noise and mayhem all around her, and sorting out who was friend or foe was harder this time because they were all human and similarly armed. The dangers of the assailants already on deck was complicated by the winged airmen still trickling in and the pulse blasts coming down from the raft-like gondola of the airship. She was fighting more by instinct than anything else. Occasionally, only her prickling senses warned that someone had targeted her, and she spun around or looked up just in time to duck an attack or blow the assailant away.

The airship was a frustration, for there seemed to be an almost infinite number of pirates aboard and at the distance it kept, she could not do anything about them or their weapons. Human bodies Zephirine was able to beat back with the winds she channeled, but the zeppelin was too large, and she didn't have the power to do more than shudder the platform and make it harder for the remaining air crew to target those on deck.

Eventually Zephirine stood at bay, partially exposed with her back against a stack of crates, holding off all the invaders she could while continually harassing the overhead menace that kept trying to shoot her down. There were just too many of them, and she was tiring, wishing very much she could take a break and recover her energy. She was not used to so much physical activity at once or the continual need to concentrate under pressure, and was becoming exhausted with all the effort.

I never wanted this! I'm no soldier! That didn't seem to matter under the current circumstances, for the enemy was more than glad to kill civilians as readily as they were taking out the crew. As her strength gave out, Zephirine could no longer stand on shaking legs. She sank to a squatting position in exhaustion, the metal supports of the rack and the corners of the crates within it digging into her back.

The situation seemed hopeless. There were just too many pirates!

The winds she called and channeled now were more of a deterrent than a weapon, and Zephirine knew she was only slowing the inevitable. She saw no one nearby she recognized, and suspected most of the crew was already dead.

Reflexes and adrenaline took over when conscious thought went numb, and she was only dimly aware of the battle raging around her. As she fought to just stay alive, her mind was reeling with the sounds of hoarse shouts, the zap and sizzle of energy weapons, rallying cries, clashing metal edges, screams of agony and despair, the thud of running feet or bodies hitting the decks, and the splash of those who went overboard. The cacophony of noises reached her ears in a chorus of dreamlike insanity. There was a crackling and the smell of smoke from burnt rope and charred flesh as Aleta passed somewhere nearby, but Zephirine was too overwhelmed to even look around and acknowledge her presence.

Channeling the wind had a physical toll, and she had never done so much of it at one time. Her muscles burned, her body shook with exhaustion, her mind only saw things through a fog, and the minutes seemed like hours. Nerves stretched tight, several times Zephirine reacted completely out of instinct when someone got too near, and she accidentally blew a couple of defenders off the boat when they were too tangled up in knots of pirate raiders charging at her. Dully, she realized she was ready for death, and was so tired of fighting; she almost welcomed the idea as she slumped down in defeat.

Several more attackers came aboard nearby as an airman with a rotten-toothed snarl of defiant triumph below his goggled mask came swooping down, his weapon ready to take someone else out. Aleta screeched as she burned the attackers on the deck away, but she was too busy to see the airman taking a bead on her. He hit her once; she staggered back, and lost her flames again.

Zephirine felt guilty about leaving her sister-in-arms fighting alone against that murderous horde, and somehow found the strength to bounce back to her feet. As tired as she was, it was gratifying to feel the rush of wind through her again, to see the airman's leather wings folding inside out, and watch him smash hard into a corner of the next stack of crates. So violent was her counterstroke that his impact split the back of his head open, and he left a bloody brains smear trail all down the crates. He slid to the deck unmoving, his charged weapon spitting pulse blasts under the rail and taking out two more of his compatriots just climbing up the side before it went into shutdown mode.

After checking on Aleta, one of the last standing defenders sprinted over and snatched the pulse rifle up, running past Zephirine to engage the butt end into the face of another pirate on his way forward, his blood-streaked face set in a grimace of defiance. Vaguely she registered that it was Shepherd the mate, yelling that he had her back before discharging the weapon into a group of attackers that were headed her way, and then he suddenly shot over her head at something. Zephirine yelped in fear as the dead body of another aerial pirate wielding a hand axe tumbled end over end, to crash-land twitching almost at her feet, smoke issuing from his mouth and ears as the inside of his electronically crisped cranium turned to liquid that seeped from his ears. Eyes rolled back into his head, his face blackened, and he twitched before going rigidly still.

She tried not to think about what kind of death that was as she directed the wind to sweep him over the rail and off the deck, his crumpled wings catching at first but ripping free with the violence of her blast.

"Ye be all right Miss Zee?" Shepherd asked, coming up to stand beside her, noting how much she was trembling. He never stopped scanning around them while he spoke to her. "Yer a mite pale and shaky. Yer not hurt or nothin'?"

"I hate this! I'm dog tired, but I'm managing," she said through gritted teeth as she blew yet another blood soaked body off the deck, not caring if it was friend or foe. "Are we going to lose the ship?"

"Not yet I daresay," he said grimly, "though it's true we're bein' overrun. I be tryin' to get to our captain, but he's somewhere aft, near as I can figure."

She turned to him with sick eyes. "He's hurt badly, lost an arm. Jordyn took him, but I don't know if he will survive."

Shepherd swore low and long without taking his eyes off the battle scene around them. "Captain Jameson's a good man. Best I ever shipped with. 'E's an old soldier. Insisted 'e had to be the one up here. Well, there's naught we can do about that now. If we could at least take out that blasted airship, t'would help; but we lost all the big guns, so none down here now has that range. Their tin bucket is 'bout useless, but the frigate be loaded with men and cannon, and if they don't take Solstice for themselves, they'll be sinking us. Those bloody caravels be just out of range too, an' they still be full o' more water rats. We need to take back the helm and move this ship forward, but I cain't get near–"

He broke off to shoot another pirate looming overhead and Zephirine blew his body away before it came down.

"We makes us a good team," Shepherd said with a cockeyed grin that she returned briefly and sidled up next to him. For all his presence used to annoy her, it was reassuring to have the bold little man at her side.

"You got hit," said Zephirine, seeing the blast burns on his face and neck.

"T'ain't nothing," he countered.

"Is Aleta still with us?" she asked suddenly, realizing she hadn't seen the small dark woman in some time.

"Aye! Last time I seen her, she was headed to stern after settin' the frigate's sails afire, trying to burn the small ships too. She's keeping them back, but she don't have the range to take them out."

That gave Zephirine an idea. "David," she said excitedly, using his given name for the first time, her hand on his arm, "If you can cover me, let's get to Aleta, because I believe I can give her the boost she needs!"

He looked at her and grinned wickedly. "You got a bit of the warrior maiden in ye after all. "Well c'mon Missy Zee, let's go help yer brave li'l lady friend roast a few more blasted pirates!"

They moved out carefully, watching all around and overhead, dodging random pulse bursts and charging madmen. The deck was awash in gory splotches and burned spots. The sickly screams, anguished cries, and moans of the injured and dying assaulted their ears. Zephirine concentrated on clearing a path ahead for them where she could, for the Solstice had few defenders left, and everywhere greedy pirates were breaking into cargo and cabins, and rifling through things.

"Hey, that's my chest!" she said as a hustling pair of men went by. Shepherd shot them where they stood, and they dragged it out of the way, shoving it into a hatchway, before going on.

Zephirine spotted Aleta first, as Shepherd was too busy, one-handedly shooting down another airman who had hit him in the shoulder with a blaster bolt, numbing the other arm to where it refused to obey for some minutes. Even so, he managed to keep up his vigilance, snatching up an abandoned blaster and using that and the pulse rifle to guard the two women as they conferred quickly in the lee of the cabins. They were more men than they had expected to see on the decks of the rapidly approaching caravels waiting for their chance to board Solstice, and they were obviously eager to get into the fight.

"We got to take them two ships out, or we won't make it through this," he said unhappily.

Aleta's spirits were also low at that point, for while she had been able to keep the caravels from snugging up and taking the stern of Solstice, she didn't have the range to reach out and burn them. Her flame throwing energy was about spent, though her fire still burned just as hot as before, and her eyes and skin glowed with it. Now that Jordyn's light had gone dim, much of the ship was bathed in sunset rays, and she was not hard to spot, so she had to keep dodging ship-to-ship weapons fire. If the fight continued much longer, they'd be in the dark and lost.

"I just can't reach them," admitted Aleta in a tired voice.

"I can," Zephirine said, "But I don't have anything powerful enough to take them out. I need you to make a fireball big enough to survive the distance and do some damage. Can you somehow manage that Aleta?"

"In my sleep," she quipped, holding her hands out and concentrating until there was a glowing mass of fire floating between them twice the size of her head. "But how are we going to get it that far away without it snuffing out? I can't keep it alive if I can't be connected to it."

"Let me worry about that," Zephirine said as they both ducked some more random pulse bursts that came their way. The shots splattered on the cabin walls behind them, leaving scorch marks in their wake. Shepherd returned fire, buying them time as Zephirine stood up and pulled together a vortex, centering the fireball within it.

"They're just at the edge of my range now, so let's see if we can deliver it and then we'll let them get a little closer for the next one," she added, releasing the vortex and sending it off with the fireball inside. It petered out right at the side of the foremost caravel, letting the fireball drop into the ocean with a hiss. The pirates shot back, and Shepherd quickly returned fire as they all ducked again.

"Stop shooting at them David, we need them to come closer," Zephirine insisted with a hand on his arm.

"They may get ye Love," he said bluntly, not caring how it sounded anymore. He had a nasty blast scar on his upper arm to match the ones on his grizzled face, but the affected shoulder was working again and he fought with a weapon in each hand.

"We'll have to risk it," Aleta said, standing to form another, bigger fireball.

"Ye two be the bravest ladies I ever been privileged to meet," he said with feeling.

"And absolutely the most desperately insane ones too, I bet," Aleta said dryly, and he chuckled.

Zephirine wound the winds around the fireball and put all the power she could harness into an intricate twist as she blew it out of Aleta's hands and at the forward caravel, which was tacking by them toward where the frigate had been tied in. The vortex riffled the sails and sent the smaller ship heeling sideways as the fireball dropped onto the deck. Immediately, nearby crewman dropped weapons and raced to beat it out.

"We have to try it again quickly," Zephirine said with growing enthusiasm as Shepherd took out an injured pirate lurching their way from the other side of the aft castle. Aleta already had the ball formed before she twisted the wind around it, and hurried to speed it on its way.

"Aim higher, for the bleedin' sails," Shepherd yelled as he waded into a brawl between several pirates and one of his nearly dead crewmen after the man tried to take back the helm. "We gotta get them boats out so's we can concentrate on getting underway!"

"Up!" Zephirine cried aloud, willing the vortex with all her might into a climbing arc. She almost had it lined up when a long range pulse blast caught her in the stomach. She doubled over and had to let it go. Too late, a distracted and nearly overwhelmed Shepherd took out the man who had shot her, but if not for Aleta tugging her coat, she would have gone head first over the stern rail.

"Damn ye to Davey Jones Locker, ye blasted sea scum," Shepherd said, frying the man to a crisp before he knelt at her side. "Can you breathe me darlin'?"

Zephirine groaned and held her arms tightly to her torso. "I'll live," she croaked out. She hoped no ribs were broken. Her entire abdomen felt as if it had been hit by the Grendel. She could barely draw enough breath, and all the nerves radiating from the area felt like they had caught fire.

"You got them!" someone yelled triumphantly from back down the deck, and there were actually a few cheers. Warning shouts came over the water as Aleta's fireball spread and a mass of flame began to flare up on the sheets of the forward caravel, fanned quickly by winds that a very weak and wobbling Zephirine directed toward it. Soon all the sails and rigging were afire and it was spreading rapidly down the mast as the pirates prepared to abandon ship, jumping into waters infested with predators of all kinds gorging themselves on fallen bodies as well as each other.

"Well done Zee, me sweet'eart," Shepherd said with a grimy-faced smile as he kissed her brow. "Oh, and you too, Miss Aleta," he added hurriedly, pecking her cheek.

And that was when Zephirine gave in to exhaustion at last, and fainted in their arms.

The True Meaning Of Life

The unearthly screech Katy Bellows let out would have been ear shattering, had anyone been able to hear it. As metallic fingers closed around the Eye of Providence, Jordyn passed within and put all the charge he could spare into the exterior. He was hoping that the touch of it alone would kill the pirate queen, but the combination of her non-biological limb and her tough, determined state somehow preserved her. The arcing mechanical arm was connected to her brain through neural sensors that provided a direct pathway for the knowledge of the ancients.

The Holy Grail of All Existence, the pure essence of the Universe, is not comprehensible to the mortal mind. In seconds she channeled all that can be known through the myriad whispers of those who had gone before, and her overloaded brain could not accept any of it. She remained alive, though her eyes rolled back into her head, as her body arched and stiffened and she began to jerk uncontrollably.

In those few moments that they shared consciousnesses, Jordyn was appalled at what an irrationally merciless but incredibly strong-willed being she was. She was determined to survive, and like a caged beast, her soul fought for freedom. He forced his way into her mind, trying to get her to give up and let the Eye take her out of this world.

Listen to the whispers, because they speak the truth. You are just one little speck in the cosmos, and the meaning of life is that life is strictly meaningless. The energy cycling of the universe is all there is or ever will be, and you are nothing to it but a means to an end. All your accomplishments are inconsequential, for you will die out here on the sea, and then be reborn and do it all over again. Let go now while you can...

"Damn you, NO! I'm not leaving yet!"

Katherine Bellows refused to give in and forced herself back to the world of the living. Though the mechanical part of the arm refused to obey, by sheer force of will she levered the fingers open, and let go of the Eye. She rolled away, groaning and gibbering incoherently, but still very much alive.

~

Zephirine could hear the echoing sounds of a man playing a harp and walking toward her, the music and footsteps overlaid with winds from every direction. She raised her head and saw she was kneeling in swirling blackness, the winking of starlight all around her. Her head reeled, and none of it made sense, but the man—a God, her mind told her—stepped forward and looked down at her.

He was not large, but still a commanding figure: blonde and fair, ageless, and his eyes had no color. A cloak whipped around him, and cross breezes played with his wild, unruly locks as he set the harp at his side, and stood with arms crossed on his bare chest.

"Arise, Daughter of the Winds. You have done well here." He offered a hand and pulled her to her feet.

"Who... are you? Where... is... this? Am I... dead?" The questions were hard to form, for part of her mind said he was a stranger, and the other part said she had always known him.

Fortunately he laughed, and bowed, kissing her hand. "Aeolus, Lord of the Winds," he said, straightening up and brushing her hair aside. "Your patron deity, Zephirine Merriwether."

"Patron Deity? How can that be? I'm not even religious!" she started to retort, but he put his fingers to his lips.

"No questions. Our time here is short. Go back and use your power to finish the battle. Take this," he said, opening a hand and giving her a pendant of a tiny silver pentacle sprouting large wings.

When she began to protest she had already done all she could, he closed her hand upon the pendant and pushed it against her heart.

"Orion is right. You are exceedingly stubborn! They still need you, so no ascendance is allowed. Wear my symbol always. If ever you doubt yourself again, touch it and think of me, and I will be with you. Now go!" Aeolus insisted, raising a hand and blowing her away, spinning through the dark until she reentered the land of the living.

~

An explosion on the port side of Solstice rocked the entire boat and boiled the sea. The Eye of Providence rolled free, and would have gone over the side, but Jordyn broke free of it again, and called it to him. He staggered, working hard to keep his footing as spray was tossed onto the deck.

Katherine Bellows slid sideways and hit the starboard rail. She scrambled to her feet, a wild light in her eyes. She pounded down the deck like a madwoman, leaping bodies and shoving people aside, shouting for her crew to abandon ship.

"Ne'er mind the blasted cargo, this tub is possessed by demons, and we're sending it to the bottom."

Vaulting over the rail, she grabbed a landing line and worked her way down to a bobbing rowboat, which would take her back out to sea. From there she could signal the airship to race in and drop the charge that would send Solstice and all left aboard to a watery grave.

"The gods will it," she kept babbling to the oarsmen. "I talked to them, and they told me." She never said which gods, and did not stop to think about that.

~

There were voices, talking to him, calling him away. He ignored them and set a charge in the canvas sling, turning it away from the frigate, with its burned sails and collapsing masts, and pointed it over the side to where the ironclad ship still snugged up against his beloved Solstice. A crowd of watchers gathered around him, the faces of the dead that had gone before. He thought he saw his father and grandfather in there, both had been seamen too. It was very confusing.

"This is still my ship, and I'm taking at least this shot," he warned them, letting the counterweight drop and watching the charge sail off and down over the side, right into one of the stacks of the Grendel. "Hit the deck," he shouted hollowly and went prostrate. No one but the spectral men heard him, not even Jordyn Orion, who was busy with the pirate queen.

The charge flew straight and true, and when the explosion came, it caught everyone by surprise. The ruptured boiler on Grendel blew a hole in her side. Low slung and heavy, she shipped water at an alarming rate. Whatever crew on board that didn't die immediately abandoned ship as it rapidly began to sink stern first.

"Got ya!" Rufus Jameson's ghost roared as Grendel upended. The host with him raised their fists and cheered as one. "Dead nuts on the first shot too! I always did have a good eye."

None save Jordyn Orion understood what happened to the pirate ship. No one came aft to congratulate the captain's victorious shot, though forever afterward the survivors would wonder just what it was that sank the ironclad Grendel. David Shepherd always swore on his honor it wasn't him.

"But where is Master Orion? And why is it so blasted cold? Why, I feel like I am light as a feather, floating away on the breeze. I can't hear you, not above the sounds of the tide coming in… I can't hear you anymore…

"No, go away! I'm not done here!" Rufus Jameson bellowed impatiently, swinging big meaty fists at the floating apparitions as they tugged at him, but they just rippled and didn't back off when he tried to bat them away.

The light around him grew brighter, becoming a long shining tunnel, just like the white light inside Orion's star. Several figures beckoned. The voice that called most insistently sounded like his old captain, the man he had first gone to sea with. There were others who had trained him. Men he had fought beside. Some who had died in his arms in the wars. Even a scarred old veteran, who with his final breath, relinquished his command to a red haired giant of a first mate. That was when Rufus Jameson knew he was no longer part of the world of the living and it was time to pass on and let another take the helm.

"All right, if it's the best way to save my ship," he grumbled as the angelic beings bore him upwards, whispering words of comfort. "You're right. Shepherd's a good man. He'll manage without me. I'm tired anyway."

His mission accomplished, Rufus Jameson was surprised to be looking down from well above the Solstice, wondering how he got there. He was not at all frightened, but felt incredibly peaceful and free; laughing when the breeze caught him and his torn and bloody clothing billowed away. Floating up into the murky skies, he bid goodbye to the ship that for twenty some odd cycles had been his home, and looked down benevolently upon the sea that had been comfort and country for his entire life. Drifting gradually away out over the ocean, he flew the fair winds like the shining gulls he used to watch as a young man who joined the Columbian Navy to fight for the freedom of the waters.

Out of sight and sound of the Solstice, the Sailor's Master of the Waters rose dripping from the waves. The blue green god smiled as he reached out and enfolded one of his own in wet and shining arms, bringing him back home to a blissful rest.

All anyone aboard Solstice felt of the captain's passing was a fresh breeze that blew away the smell of char and death for a moment and tantalized with the nearness of land and safe harbor.

~

"She's coming to," Aleta said grimly to Shepherd, as she helped him get a still breathless and shaken Zephirine back onto her feet after she began to stir.

"I…I'm all right," Zephirine said, wobbly but upright again. In her hand was something on a chain that she half remembered accepting, but wasn't sure if it was a dream. She tucked it into a pocket. "Where do we stand?"

"One caravel down, one to go," Shepherd answered, but then looked up as something flew overhead, making a whistling noise as it arced down toward the water.

There was a loud rattling from somewhere to port and then a ship-rocking explosion that lit up the dusk sky and slopped the water.

They all went prone, expecting to be blown to bits, thinking the reactor core must have overloaded at last. But with a sense of triumph a moment later, they realized it was the Grendel's engines that had ruptured, as the ironclad ship began to upend and sink beneath the waves.

"Ladies, try and get that other ship!" Shepherd shouted over his shoulder as he raced to the port side with the pulse rifle set to its highest level. "I gotta cut that hunk of iron free so's she don't heel us over as she goes down."

He blasted the landing lines and part of the railing free, noting the pirates were vacating Solstice, leaving most of their plunder behind. The airship circled to gain altitude, where it would be high and out of range. Looking up, Shepherd saw an ominous shape being reeled along the gondola platform.

Without warning, Jordyn Orion stood beside him, watching Goliath ponderously making its circuit before coming in.

"They plan to sink us," Shepherd said grimly. "And the bleedin' thing is out of range of me blasted rifle."

"I have something to show you that might reach it," Jordyn said grabbing his arm, "But it's up there, and you have to hurry!"

Shepherd handed Jordyn his weapon and raced for the stairs, taking them two and three at a time.

Jordyn tossed the pulse rifle aside and teleported past Aleta and Zephirine, who were taking on the last of the caravels with another airborne fireball. He stood atop the weather deck beside Shepherd, explaining just how the small contrived trebuchet was going to be very instrumental in delivering a final message that piracy was not as profitable as it used to be.

"And Capt'n Jameson showed you all this 'fore he died?" the wild eyed mate asked as he loaded a wad of explosive gum with a detonator and set it in the sling.

"He was a brave and honorable man," Jordyn answered as they watched the charge fly off.

～

They would talk about it for ages. How the good ship Solstice, with a skeleton crew and three passengers, fought off a horde of bloodthirsty cutthroats. People in waterfront towns spoke in hushed and reverent tones of how as in the tales of old, a small man named David Shepherd stood alone on the weather deck and, using a sling and a stone of fire, blew giant Goliath out of the sky.

The explosion and resulting fireball were seen and heard for hundreds of miles as the big airship burned. It was fortunate that the winds shifted and blew it all out to sea. The story, filled with heroic deeds and poignant sacrifices, would be retold for generations to come.

Somehow, that single incident was the catalyst that put the heart back into a hopeless people who had seen much hardship and warmongering, privation and dread times. Maybe there was a chance for the world of humankind after all, if a half dead ship with a handful of people aboard could survive such an ordeal.

When they finally arrived on Columbiana's rocky coast after being ferried from the docking point at New Brooklyn Harbor, Jordyn, Aleta, and Zephirine were cheered and greeted with a heroes' welcome from a shoreline town full of poor people barely eking out any existence they could muster.

～

Two sets of eyes watched the trio ferried in, both creatures of the tide.

One glared from a row boat, wrapped in an old cloak that hid her now dead mechanical arm. Her brown eyes burned with malevolent hatred. She spat in the water, swearing an oath, demanding that the men row her back out to a leaking frigate with hastily rigged sails.

The other eyes were brown too, but male. Calm and curious, his freckled furry body held his head bobbing just above the lapping tide. He noted how the strange people were given a hero's welcome. Two of them were pretty land walker ladies, though a bit worse for wear.

The other was something else…

There were hunters around with their seal guns, and so he flipped and dove beneath the waves, heading back to his lonely rocky island until nighttime, when he could slip into town and see what could be seen.

THE END

About Our Creators

AUTHOR—

NANCY HANSEN - An avid reader and prolific writer of fantasy and adventure fiction for over 25 years, Nancy A. Hansen is the author of the novels FORTUNE'S PAWN, PROPHECY'S GAMBIT, MASTER'S ENDGAME, and FORGED BY FLAME, anthologies TALES OF THE VAGABOND BARDS, THE HUNTRESS OF GREENWOOD, and THE WINDRIDERS OF EVERICE, novellas COMPANION DRAGON'S TALES: *A FAMILIAR NAME, COPPER'S CHOICE,* and co-author of *FINDING WAXY.* Her short stories have been featured in multiple issues of Pro Se Presents, and she has a tale each in Pro Se Anthologies THE NEW ADVENTURES OF SENORITA SCORPION, TALL PULP, THE NEW ADVENTURES OF THE WHIRLWIND, MONSTER ACES #2, and SINGULARITY: RISE OF THE POSTHUMANS. while the E-story TO RULE THE SKY is offered as a Pro Se SINGLE SHOT. Nancy has contributed stories to both Airship 27's SINBAD: THE NEW VOYAGES Volume 1 and Mechanoid Press' debut book, MONSTER EARTH, as well as the charity anthologies LEGENDS OF NEW PULP and THE LOST CHILDREN. She is also the author of the Airship 27 pirate series, JEZEBEL JOHNSTON. Nancy currently resides on an old farm in beautiful, rural eastern Connecticut with an eclectic cast of family members, and one very spoiled dog.

ARTIST—

G.S.DAVIS - is an artist hailing from the wilds of Arvada. At the tender age of 15, he discovered that his calling was storytelling. Naturally he discovered this talent while trying to get out of trouble with his mother. As time went on, he evolved his talent and soon began writing comics. Now, many years later, he's still trying to avoid getting in trouble, though he believes that his wife is probably on to him at this point. So he tends to hide in his office, writing comics and putting them out into the world. He draws in two different styles: A cartoon style distantly reminiscent of the newspaper strips of yore, and a more serious Manga style, distantly reminiscent of Japanese comic books from that far away land.

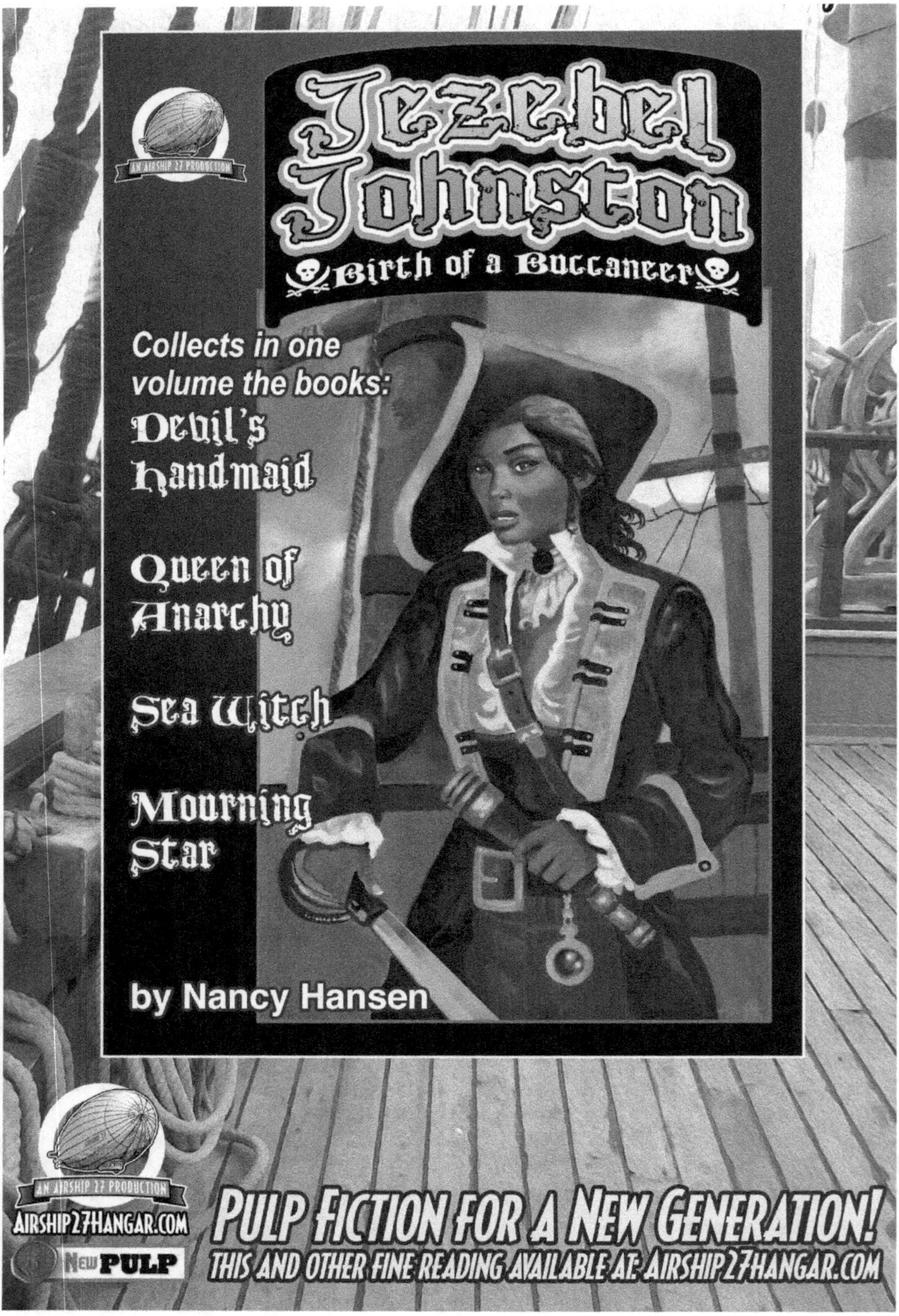
AN AIRSHIP 27 PRODUCTION
Jezebel Johnston
Birth of a Buccaneer
Collects in one volume the books:
Devil's Handmaid
Queen of Anarchy
Sea Witch
Mourning Star
by Nancy Hansen
AN AIRSHIP 27 PRODUCTION
AIRSHIP27HANGAR.COM
NEW PULP
PULP FICTION FOR A NEW GENERATION!
THIS AND OTHER FINE READING AVAILABLE AT: AIRSHIP27HANGAR.COM

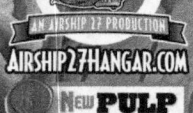

www.ingramcontent.com/pod-product-compliance
Lightning Source LLC
Chambersburg PA
CBHW070813250626
47170CB00006B/2092